A LOVE CONCEALED

MARY'S LADIES, BOOK 3

BELLE MCINNES

Eden
Press

Printed in the United Kingdom
First published, 2020
Cover by Alba Covers

Find out more about Belle and her upcoming books by joining her newsletter:
https://www.subscribepage.com/joinbelle

Mary Queen of Scots is on the throne, but villainous plotters have designs on her throne...

Held captive during her teens by an evil lord, beautiful heiress Margaret Carwood uses her wits and ingenuity to escape his clutches, becoming Mary Queen of Scots' favoured lady-in-waiting in the process.

With her future secure, she's fiercely determined never to be dominated by a man again, and convinced that she doesn't need to marry to be happy. Until she meets Highland laird, John Stewart…

MAP

SCOTLAND IN THE TIME OF MARY QUEEN OF SCOTS

CHAPTER 1

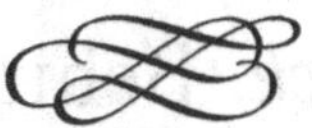

WEDNESDAY 4TH DECEMBER 1566

Margaret Carwood rammed her fists onto her hips and raised her chin. "Who do you think you are, sire, to claim the part of the king?" she demanded.

"Only his direct descendant, my lady," replied the laird of Fincastle, lifting a well-muscled shoulder. Sat on a window seat in an alcove formed by the depth of the thick stone walls of Craigmillar Castle, John Stewart of Tulliepowries appeared unconcerned by the great honour he was asking. "Robert the

Bruce was my great-grandfather's great-grandfather's great-great-grandfather. So it seems only right that I should play him."

Yes, but I'll bet The Bruce never had eyes so blue nor hair so black. Behind Margaret, a fire burned in the wide fireplace of the great hall. But the glowing logs only served to take the worst of the chill from the November air. Outside, the sky was filled with clouds the colour of steel and a merciless wind whistled up the hill from Little France, buffeting off the castle's curtain wall and swirling around the high tower.

Clenching her jaw, Margaret turned her back on the Highlander and addressed Sebastian Pages, who acted as master of ceremonies to Mary Queen of Scots and directed all her masques. "What say you, Bastian? Should we allow this man to take the lead part? 'Twould be his first role here at Craigmillar, and he's arrived but five minutes.

Quite a coup for a laird newly come to court!"

The Frenchman rubbed his chin, eyeing the well-built laird with his broad chest and square jaw. "But they are hardly queueing out of the door to join us. Let him audition for the part by rehearsing with us this afternoon. If he can act, good. If he cannot, then I can step in. I wrote the words, after all. But The Bruce was tall and strong, and," Bastian waved a hand at his slim figure, encased in a blue doublet and matching trunk hose, "much as I would wish to claim those attributes, I am not."

He thrust a sheaf of papers at the Highlander. "These are the lines. We will rehearse the third scene." Giving Margaret a sideways look, he added, "That will let us see if he can *really* act."

Margaret's chest constricted. "But..." Scene three was the love tryst. She would have to kiss the laird, a man she didn't even know. "I cannot—"

Waving his fingers at her, Bastian dismissed her protests. "We all know that you are a talented actress, Lady Carwood. This should be easy for you. 'Tis the Highlander who will find it difficult."

~

In the grey winter light that filtered through the leaded windows, John Stewart of Tulliepowries and third Laird Fincastle leafed through the hand-written script, his heart sinking.

Scene three had The Bruce bidding farewell to his wife on his way to confront the English. With her flame-coloured hair and her heart-shaped face Lady Carwood might be beautiful, but she had a tongue on her as sharp as the edge of a broadsword and a fiery personality that matched her hair. Not the lady he would have chosen to kiss.

Unfolding his long legs, he stepped from the window embrasure. If he wanted to rebuild his castle, he needed his inheritance. And that wouldn't happen if he didn't get his name known at court. What better way to do that than as leading man in a play for the queen? He clenched his jaw. *Best get it over and done wi'.* Addressing the others, he said, "I'm ready."

Bastian shepherded him to a spot at the back of the hall, at the opposite end to the great fireplace where the queen would sit to watch their masque. "You are about to lead your country to war against the English. If all goes well, you will be a hero. But if it goes badly, you will never see your wife, Elizabeth de Burgh, again." He pointed at a spot two paces to John's right. "There is your mark. And here—" he indicated a dark shadow on the flagstone floor, "is yours, Lady Carwood.

You know what you have to do. With this scene, we want to make them cry."

With sadness, I presume, no' tears of laughter, John thought with a wry smile, standing at his appointed place, half-facing forward, and half towards Lady Carwood.

Taking a deep breath, he focussed his mind on the woman in front of him, imagining how he'd have felt if he'd had to bid farewell to his Lizzy. Just the thought of it made his throat thicken and his chest swell. If only he could have told her, one more time, how much she meant to him…

Swallowing, he took Lady Carwood's hand and started to read from the script. "Elizabeth, dear heart, we go in search of the English the 'morn." He kissed her hand and looked into her blue-grey eyes. "Will ye wait for me?"

"Aye, and I shall pray for ye too, sire," replied Lady Carwood, taking a step closer so they were only a hands-width apart.

With the rustle of her garments came the scent of vanilla, making his nostrils flare. In the dim light from the candle sconces her green eyes gleamed like lustrous emeralds. *She really is breath-taking.* 'Twas a shame she was more prickly than a hedgehog.

He cleared his throat, and dropped his eyes to the script. "Edward's army are camped to the south, and my scouts say they have twice our numbers. But we are fighting for our land, and for our freedom!" He softened his voice again, and added some warmth to the next words. "And I will be fighting for you, my love. Give me a token of your affections that I can take into battle with me."

A slim finger rose to his cheek, and traced the line of his jaw. "I will give you more than a token," she whispered.

For a moment, John was unable to breathe. Without checking the script for his next lines, he responded instinctively, dropping his mouth to hers and drawing her into his arms.

For a moment, he forgot they had an audience. The soft bud of her lips was like a flower that opened at his touch, her mouth sweet like honey, her body pliant in his arms.

And for a moment, he disregarded Lady Carwood's aggravating personality. Instead, he enjoyed the memories evoked by the comely woman in his arms, reminders of a time past; a time when he had a woman to warm his bed, set a fire in his loins, and kindle love in his heart.

With a cry, the Highlander thrust Margaret away from him, the look of anguish on his face so fleeting she wondered afterwards if she'd imagined it. But her racing pulse told a different story. *What just happened?* Clenching her fists, Margaret filled her lungs, hoping the deep draught of air would calm her breathing and settle her churning thoughts.

In front of her, Laird Fincastle quickly slipped a mask of impassivity into place, and his jaw tightened as he dropped his head to scan his lines.

Clearing his throat, he returned to the words Bastian had composed for the masque. Blue eyes calm now, he touched his chest, then held out his hands. "Ye have my heart, Elizabeth. Keep it safe till we meet again."

Margaret straightened her back, quieting her mind so she could focus once more on the part she had to play. With her heart rate almost back to normal, she put her hands over his, meeting his earnest gaze. "Always."

They stood like that for several seconds, frozen in a tableau, before a shout of, "Bravo!" broke the spell and they sprang apart.

Bastian came towards them, clapping

wildly, his face wreathed in smiles. "Bravo!" he repeated, grasping the Highlander by the shoulder. "It appears you *can* act, Laird Fincastle. My faith in you was justified." He stabbed his forefinger at the sheaf of papers in his hand. "Learn your lines, and we will rehearse again on the morrow. Ten o'clock. I will get the rest of the cast to join us so we can run through every scene. We only have three days till the queen leaves Craigmillar, and I want us to be word-perfect by then!"

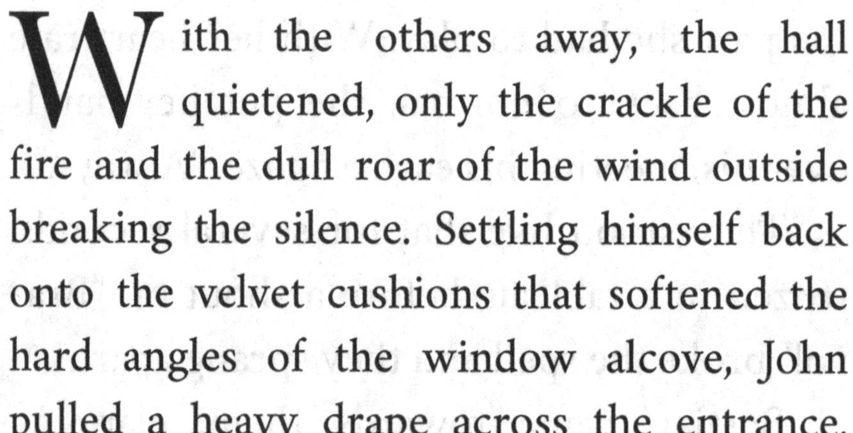

With the others away, the hall quietened, only the crackle of the fire and the dull roar of the wind outside breaking the silence. Settling himself back onto the velvet cushions that softened the hard angles of the window alcove, John pulled a heavy drape across the entrance, shutting out the rest of the world so he could concentrate on Bastian's script.

It would be an honour to play his ancestor, as Lady Carwood had implied. What man with a brave heart and a modicum of talent could pass up a chance like that? Robert the Bruce had lived a life of legend, and the history the Frenchman had used to create his masque was dramatic and compelling. However, it would not be easy to learn all of these lines by tomorrow. He wouldn't have time for anything else.

Immersed in the stories of The Bruce's wranglings with King Edward of England, Robert didn't immediately notice that others had entered the hall. And because he was hidden from sight, silently reading in his window seat, the incomers were also unaware of his presence. It was only when their voices rose in disagreement that John's head jerked up and his attention focussed on the meeting that was taking place beyond his hiding place, rather than the words of the Frenchman's play.

"Fire or poison. 'Tis the only way," said a gruff voice, a hint of anger evident in his clipped tone. "Even in the hands of a marksman, a gun cannot be relied upon."

"But the queen was suspicious of poisoning at Jedburgh," said another, in lighter tones.

"She suspected arson there too, if you remember." This man's voice was lower-pitched, with the guttural brogue of the north-east. "But however we do it, Her Grace needs rid of him."

John's skin chilled at those words. *They speak of the queen!* But who would they be rid of?

"But not in a way that would harm Prince James' succession." An older man spoke those words, his tone measured and his words precise. "The queen would not allow that."

Surely they could not mean to be rid of the king? John's breathing quickened. *That would be treason!*

Yesterday, not long after he had arrived at Craigmillar, John had caught a brief glimpse of the king, Henry Stewart, Lord Darnley, just hours before he left, supposedly for Stirling Castle. A cousin of the queen—and probably some distant cousin of John's, since they shared a surname and ancestry dating back to Robert the Bruce—Darnley was tall and handsome, with fair hair and a slim figure.

But his fine looks were deceptive, for the king had gained a reputation as a dissolute drunkard who frequented the taverns and whorehouses of Edinburgh rather than his wife's bed. And rumours at court had it that Darnley was, even now, sailing for Spain to raise an army in support of his claim to the throne.

John shook his head. Regardless of his

failings, could these men really mean to be rid of the *king*? That would be regicide, and a sure route to the gallows.

"The queen would not allow *this*," a more refined voice interjected, his tone nasal, "if she but knew."

"So she must not know," said the older man again, and paused. "It must be between us, and us alone." Those last words were spoken more slowly, as if he looked each one in the eye.

"You forget the bastard," said the fierce one. "'Twas his idea."

"Mmm." John could almost hear the wheels turning in the older man's brain. "But Moray is away right now."

"Conveniently," commented a fifth man with a rich, deep voice that John had not heard until this moment.

They spoke of the queen's half-brother, the earl of Moray. If this was a conspiracy, as it appeared to be, John found it hard to believe that Mary's flesh and blood would join a plot that would impact her throne.

"Mayhap. But he will support us in this. He has given his word." There was a creaking of wood, as if the older man sat in one of the oak chairs that surrounded the banqueting tables. "Now, do I have your bond of silence? For if even a hint gets out, they will have us hanged."

"Or exiled," the haughtier voice sniffed. "Morton has still not been allowed to return to Scotland."

The older man drew air through his teeth. "So we must be sure that nobody else knows of our plans."

In the silence that followed, John's nose began to itch, and his eyes started to water as dust from the draperies threatened to make him sneeze. *Damn my weak lungs!* His throat dry, he pinched his nostrils with his left hand, the other hand clasping the hilt of his sword. *If they find me, I'm dead.*

As if to confirm his fear, the next words from the angry lord caused John's heart to stop. "If any suspect, they must die." There was a ring of steel as the speaker drew his weapon. "And if any here betray us..." The glint of his blade must have been sufficient threat that he didn't need to finish the sentence.

But John was in agony. The itch in his nostrils had built to an unbearable pressure, and his discovery was imminent. *I'll have to fight my way out,* he thought, just as the sneeze escaped and all hell broke loose...

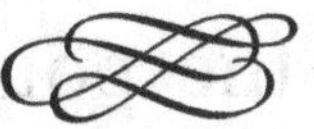

CHAPTER 2

Mary eyed her lady-in-waiting. Lady Carwood's skin had an unusual flush, and her movements were less assured than normal as she inspected the white soup and veal flory stew that had been sent up for the queen's luncheon.

A wave of apprehension flooded through the queen's chest, and she put a hand on Margaret's arm. "Is something wrong, Lady Carwood? 'Ave you concern about the food?" Even though she'd been in Scotland for five years, when she was anxious, Mary's accent became stronger and this made her French upbringing more evident.

"No ma'am."

So it was not the poisoner again. Mary glanced around the salon. There was nobody else within earshot. "But you do not seem yourself. Has something happened?"

Margaret's hesitation was an answer in itself.

"Something is wrong. Tell me," Mary demanded, all thoughts of food forgotten, for Margaret was her favourite companion, only recently returned to court from her sister's household in Biggar. "Is it Janet? Or her baby?"

"No, no, my sister is fine, last I heard. And the bairn too."

"Does Laird Persellands treat her well?"

Margaret's mouth turned down. "Not the way I would want to be treated. It still vexes me that she had to marry that beast." She wrinkled her nose. "I know not how she could countenance having a baby with him."

Mary put a hand on her lady-in-waiting's arm. "You will change your mind, my dear Margaret, when you find a husband of your own."

"That will never happen." Margaret's tone was decisive.

"So you say." Mary quirked her brow. "But you know that I intend to find you an handsome lord, one who will dispel your hatred of men and convince you of the joys of matrimony."

"From what I have seen of my brother-in-law, and, if I may say it, of your own husband, Lord Darnley, matrimony does not seem such a joy."

Margaret's forthrightness was one of the qualities Mary liked in the young woman, but sometimes her honesty hit a raw nerve. "Remember, you speak of the king," the queen chided. Then she softened her expression. "Do not let any others hear you talk so, for if they hear opinions like that from you, my dear, they will think that those are also the queen's thoughts."

"And are they not? Do I not speak the truth?"

Her fists clenched and her chest tight, Mary stepped to the window, looking out over the formal gardens to the south of the castle, with their box hedges and the pretentious pond in the shape of a 'P' that Laird Preston had designed to signify his family name. "Whatever I think, 'tis of no import. For we are married in the eyes of God, and I cannot divorce Darnley if I want Prince James to be my legitimate heir."

Mary watched a brown-clad servant lead two lanky deerhounds along the path that bordered the castle walls. "When we were in Jedburgh, Maitland said he would petition the Pope, but," her shoulders drooped, "there is no way out, without disadvantaging my son."

"And still you think I should marry?" Margaret's tone was kinder.

Mary spun around, and took her lady-in-waiting's hands. "Yes! For you will make a better choice than I. Your experiences at Biggar will see to that. And I will help you. I will find you a fine man who will make your heart beat faster."

Margaret paused briefly, then pursed her lips. "Methinks that might take you forever, ma'am. But before you tax yourself acting as matchmaker, mayhap you should take some sustenance," she pointed at the soup, "and I will look over my lines for the masque. Oh!" Her hand flew to her mouth.

"What is amiss?" Mary narrowed her eyes. Would she finally discover the cause of Margaret's agitation?

"My script! I must have left it in the hall." Margaret bobbed a curtsey. "Would you excuse me for a few moments, ma'am, till I fetch it?"

With a roar, James Hepburn, the Earl of Bothwell, rushed across the great hall and threw back the wall-hangings, revealing a black-haired Highlander skulking in the window recess, plaid thrown over his shoulder and sword half-drawn. "Who have we here?" he snarled, pointing his sword at the man's heart. "A spy?"

The eavesdropper pushed his own weapon back into its sheath and showed his palms. "No sir. Merely a man who was reading quietly in the window seat," he indicated a pile of papers lying on the cushion behind him, "only to be disturbed by your voices." He straightened his shoulders and looked Bothwell in the eye. "I am John Stewart of Tulliepowries, Laird of Fincastle.

And I am someone who might have a solution to your—" his lips narrowed, "—little problem."

"I am not interested in your solutions," Bothwell growled. "It only proves that you heard too much and are a threat to us." Glancing over his shoulder, he kept his arm rock-steady and the tip of his sword resting on Fincastle's chest. He was pleased to see that the earls of Huntly and Argyll were also facing the intruder with their weapons drawn. "What say you, my lords?"

"I agree. We cannot afford for our plans to be known," said George Gordon, the Earl of Huntly.

"Even if I can provide a fail-safe way for you to be rid of someone who is an inconvenience?" interjected the Highlander, with a lift of an eyebrow.

Who was this man, who did not seem to care for the danger he was in? "Why should we—"

Bothwell was interrupted by William Maitland of Lethington, the queen's secretary, who had a calculating look in his eye. "Fail-safe, you say?"

"Aye," replied Fincastle, "although not wi'out risk."

"Any method will have its risks." Maitland smoothed his beard with finger and thumb. "Tell us more about what you propose."

Fincastle stared pointedly at Bothwell's sword. "If I am to trust ye with my suggestion, 'twould be appreciated if ye could return some o' that trust."

Maitland waved a hand at the Earl. "Give Fincastle a little leeway, Lord Bothwell. He is outnumbered, and well he knows it. But let us hear what he has to say."

Reluctantly, Bothwell took a step backwards, lowering his sword. "Speak, then," he said, jerking his chin at the Highlander.

Fincastle inclined his head. "If ye know

my estates in Perthshire, ye will know that I own limekilns. And a limestone quarry." He said this last with grave importance, as if it was of some significance.

"And what matter is that?"

"We excavate the rock using gunpowder. Which I import regularly from Flanders."

In the brief silence that followed, Maitland touched his fingertips together, then tilted his head at Fincastle. "You propose an explosion?"

"Aye." The laird hooked a thumb into his belt. "In the right circumstances it can be deadly."

"But," Bothwell raised the tip of his sword to add menace to his words, "why would you help us, sire? You do not know us." Narrowing his eyes, he added, "Nor we you. You could betray us at any moment." He turned to the others. "My lords, we agreed that our plans had to stay secret. We cannot trust this

—" he flicked a hand at the Highlander, "— northern limmer."

"On the contrary, my lord." Fincastle lifted a corner of his mouth in a lopsided grin. "I have every reason to support you. Like our queen, saints preserve her, I am descended from Robert the Bruce, although my ancestor was a bastard son of The Wolf of Badenoch so I have no claim to the throne. But I have heard that the king plans to raise an army with the help of the Spanish, to depose Mary. So I would be glad to serve any cause that will keep our rightful sovereign safe."

"What say you, gentlemen?" Maitland's hooded gaze swept the room. "Shall we trust this Fincastle?"

A clatter of boots on flagstone signalled that the men inside approached the studded oak door of the great hall. Margaret, who had been crouched outside hardly believing what she was hearing, scuttled into the side pantry and fussed with some plates as if preparing something for the queen.

Holding her breath, she willed her pulse to slow, rather than pounding as loud as a mummer's drum. The thickness of the great hall door had prevented her from hearing all but the loudest voices, but she had heard talk of the queen, an explosion, and secret plans.

Worse, in amongst the other voices she had heard the Highland brogue of the Laird of Fincastle, who would play her husband in the masque in two night's time. So he was a knave, just like all other men. And one of the plotters. *I should have known.*

Her stomach churning, she ducked low as

the men dispersed, thundering down the spiral staircase to the courtyard below.

I must tell Her Grace. But would the queen believe her? For one of the voices had been that of Mary's most trusted protector, the Earl of Bothwell. And from her hiding place in the pantry she had recognised the measured tread of Sir William Maitland, the queen's secretary, another man who had the queen's confidence.

But why would they plot against her mistress, when she had been so good to them? Margaret stilled for a moment, then scolded herself. How could she forget the evil conspirators who murdered poor Riccio, and almost killed the queen?

All the men surrounding the queen craved her power, regardless of the cost. It appeared that even loyal Bothwell had been seduced by the lure of the throne, after proving himself the queen's most steadfast lord for many years.

Fussing with some misaligned goblets for the sole purpose of keeping her hands busy, Margaret heaved a deep sigh. It seemed that even the best of supporters could not be relied upon.

But why would she be surprised at the evil perpetrated by men? For did she not have first-hand evidence of the deceitfulness and depravity of the sons of Adam, after growing up under the guardianship of Laird Persellands?

Appointed guardian after their parents drowned, their uncle had squandered the family fortune and sequestered their lands, rather than preserving the estates and properties entrusted to him.

Then he had added insult to injury by forcing Janet to marry him. He was a beast. And Fincastle and the others had just proven that they were no better.

Margaret clenched her jaw. She would need to get evidence before she could tell the queen. Otherwise Maitland would worm his way out of any accusation with some clever words, and Bothwell would charm the queen so she would believe no ill of him.

Her mind made up, and the corridor outside now quiet, Margaret carefully slipped out of the pantry and stepped through the open door into the great hall. Spying the papers of her script lying on a banqueting table near the fireplace, she hurried across the cavernous room, her footsteps pattering lightly over the rush mats which covered the cold grey flagstones.

"Lady Carwood!"

For a moment, Margaret thought that a ghost had spoken her name, for she could see no-one, and a chill ran down her spine. Clutching her chest, she scanned the room, then startled when Fincastle appeared from the window seat. A flush rose up her cheeks.

She ducked a quick curtsey to hide her embarrassment. "Laird Fincastle."

"Please, call me John," he said with a nod of acknowledgement. "If I'm to play your husband in the masque, it seems wrong for us to be so formal wi' each other."

Margaret drew herself to her full height, and flared her nostrils. "Nevertheless, I prefer the formality, sire. It makes things easier, here at court—as you will discover."

"Do you no' address your friends by their given names?"

Picking up her script, Margaret patted the edges of the sheaf with the side of her hand, lining up the papers. "Indeed I do," she said, raising her chin, but refusing to give him the answer he was looking for.

Fincastle took a step closer, his mouth curling up at the side. In the wan light of the north-facing window, his blue eyes had a smoky intensity that made her heart beat faster, despite the disdain she felt for him and his fellow plotters. "And can we no' be friends, my lady? I am new here at court, so I could sore do wi' an ally to advise me and keep me from making a fool o' mysel'. And you have the ear of the queen. So if I *do* tread on toes in my uncouth ignorance, mayhap you could smooth things over for me?"

Margaret dragged her eyes away from his handsome face, and dropped her head, pretending to examine her script. She was about to tell him that she saved her favours for those who deserved them, when a thought struck her. *Yes. That is what I should do.* She raised her gaze to meet his again. "Mayhap I could." She forced the corners of her lips into a tiny smile, concealing her distaste for him and his duplicity. "John," she added carefully.

The laird's face lit up as if the sun had suddenly appeared from behind a cloud. "And may I call you Margaret?"

With an effort of will, she inclined her head. *Until I find out why you are plotting against my mistress.* Then it would be the dungeons for him and his fellow conspirators. She tucked her script under her arm. "But now I must learn my lines."

"As must I." He gave a small bow. "Good day to you, my lady."

She softened a knee and gave him a tiny curtsey. "And to you, sire."

For now, she would pretend to be his friend, get close to him, and gain his confidence. As Bastian had said, she was a good actress. She could surely get him to believe that she liked him; beguile him if need be. She would grit her teeth and quash the repugnance she felt. Although… the fact that he was not ugly would make it easier, even if he *was* a knave.

Once she had his confidence, she would discover his secrets, and use that information to save the queen from whatever nefarious scheme he and the other lords were concocting.

She turned for the door. *I will keep Her Grace safe,* she resolved. *I, Margaret Carwood, and I alone.*

All the guards and armies at Holyrood had been of no help in March when a gang of treasonous lords had burst into Mary's chamber to kill her Italian secretary. Then, two nights later, Margaret had been one of those who helped the queen to escape to the safety of Dunbar Castle, from where she was able to raise an army large enough to convince the perpetrators that self-imposed exile was their safest choice.

I am her trusted lady-in-waiting, and I shall show her that she needs no other, Margaret thought, squaring her shoulders as she pushed open the studded oak door. *I will give my life for her, if need be.*

Hands on his hips, John watched Lady Carwood's narrow back almost quiver with pride as she stalked across the hall. *Well. That was an agreement hard won.* He had fully expected her to rebuff his advances, and leave him with his head in his hands and a flea in his ear. But, surprisingly, she had agreed to be friends. He smiled to himself. Mayhap she was not so prickly as he first thought.

And he truly wished for them to be friends, not just because she was comely and fair of face. No, now that he had inveigled himself into the plot against the king, he needed someone with the ear of the queen who could pass on a warning, and speak on his behalf once he knew the exact nature of the scheme the lords were devising. Margaret would be an ideal accomplice, if only he could gain her trust.

Until then, and until the plot was agreed and he could send warning to the king, he needed to keep his eyes open and his wits about him, or it could end up being *him* who was done away with, not the king. He came close to it, just then. Only fast talking and even faster thinking had saved him from being speared like a stuck pig on the end of Bothwell's sword.

He would need fast thinking, too, when negotiating the formalities and politics of court. And, as if this was not difficult enough, John now had to spy on the plotters without getting himself killed or implicated in their treason. No mean feat for a simple sheep farmer from Perthshire!

The thought made him grimace. But he needed to stay the course, so he could meet the terms of his father's will and find a wife.

In the meantime, he had lines to learn for Bastian's masque. T'would not do to be left gaping wordless like a beached trout in front of the queen and her nobles.

Even worse to be left stuttering in front of Lady Carwood. *Already I have felt her ire more times than I care for.* Instead, he needed to gain her confidence and change her opinion of him.

He smiled to himself. With luck, this play would give him the perfect opportunity.

~

It was the tryst scene that convinced her.

From her ornately-carved oak chair, set pride of place before the makeshift stage in the great hall, Mary narrowed her eyes.

There was some strange energy between those two. The handsome Highland laird, with his hair curling black on his shoulders and his intense stare was a perfect counterpoint to the flame-haired lady-in-waiting with her milk-white skin and spirited temperament.

He will be ideal for Margaret! Mary would have to play matchmaker for those two. Although, if the simmering passions when they played Bruce's farewell were anything to go by, mayhap Mary would need to do little to push them together.

Perhaps they were already courting. She would need to quiz Margaret. Perhaps her companion had been keeping secrets, and that was what had her all a-fluster at lunchtime on Wednesday.

With a change of scenery, the masque moved forward to the scene where Bruce and his army won a resounding victory over the English. Similarly, Mary's thoughts moved to the personal battles she faced.

On the morrow, she would travel to Holyrood, and thence to Stirling, to prepare for Prince James' christening later in the month. But her stomach tied in knots every time she thought of it, for after their last fight, her feckless husband had stormed off, purportedly to Stirling.

Mary had been incensed when she discovered, later, that Darnley had actually ridden to Dunbar, intending to travel to the continent and petition the Spanish king to raise a Catholic army in support of his claim to the Scottish crown.

Intervention by the French ambassador, Monsieur du Croc, had dissuaded him—for the moment—but it was still unclear whether the king would attend the baptism in Stirling, or whether in his pique he would refuse to participate in the ceremony.

Perhaps she should not have refused him when he asked to join her in her bedchamber on Monday night. But with the rumours of his whoring and licentiousness... It was hard to look him in the eye. And the idea of him touching her... Mary shuddered.

Up on the stage, the performers had reached the final scene of the masque. A triumphant Bruce attached his royal seal to a peace treaty where the English acknowledged Scotland as an independent country and Bruce and his heirs—of which Mary was the most recent—as rightful rulers of Scotland.

As Fincastle and the other actors stood frozen in their final tableau, Mary inclined her head in acknowledgement, then led the applause. Around her, the patriotic audience clapped and cheered, feet stamping on the flagstones and whistles ringing around the rafters.

But that final scene had given Mary an idea of how she should deal with Darnley, and a weight slipped from her shoulders. *It might work,* she thought, and smiled grimly. She would put things in motion when they reached Stirling.

CHAPTER 3

SATURDAY 7TH DECEMBER 1566

Margaret watched from her vantage point at the entrance to the inner curtilage of Craigmillar Castle. From the stables appeared a pretty chestnut mare with a chalky star on her forehead, and legs that were white from the knees down, making the horse look like she wore gleaming, silvery hose.

The mare was on her toes, snorting worriedly at the large crowd of riders and pack horses that were assembled in the outer courtyard of the castle, breath misting in the chilly air. Seconds later, the mare almost pulled the crooked little groom who led her off his feet. Margaret looked questioningly at Mary.

"This is Ember, one of my new horses," said the queen. "A ride like this is just what she needs, I think. 'Twill calm her, let her see something of the world. Especially with a horsewoman such as you riding her." With a gracious smile, Mary acknowledged the compliment she gave Margaret. "And then next week after the long ride to Stirling she will settle, and I shall send her to Alexandra, to finish her training."

So I am to ride a horse that is only partially trained, thought Margaret as she walked towards her mount, noticing that it took two stablehands to get the mare to stand by the stone steps that acted as a mounting block.

'Twas just as well she learned to ride as a toddler, and followed her father's hounds almost every week. She held her peace, gritted her teeth and carefully slid a leg over the saddle, settling quietly onto the mare's back.

Immediately she felt the weight of a rider, Ember tensed the muscles alongside her spine, and a fleeting vision ran through Margaret's mind of the mare bouncing around the courtyard with her head between her knees and her spine arched like a bow, while Margaret sailed unceremoniously through the air. *Not in my best navy riding habit!*

The thought of landing in the mud with all the courtiers laughing at her inspired Margaret to action. Quickly, she turned the mare in a small circle that would prevent her from bucking, until her back softened and her muscles relaxed. "Good girl," she said, risking taking one hand off the reins to pat the mare's shoulder.

"I will send Laird Fincastle to ride with you," said Mary from a few yards away as she mounted her favourite grey palfrey. "His horse is a big steady hunter who will be a good influence on Ember."

Was it Margaret's imagination, or was there a glint in the queen's eye as she said that? *Surely not.*

A moment later, a heavy-boned black horse appeared beside them. "Good morning, Lady Carwood," said Laird Fincastle, removing a black velvet cap adorned with a ruby brooch and a dashing white feather. A raven curl escaped when he replaced the hat, trailing carelessly across a high cheekbone. "It seems I am to accompany you."

Margaret was about to tell him that she'd be fine on her own, when she remembered her resolve to get closer to the Highlander. There had been no opportunity last night at the feast that followed their masque—which had received a standing ovation—and the days before that had been full of rehearsals and costume-making. With a dip of her head, she acknowledged his presence. "Thank you, sire."

"Bastian tells me there is to be another masque at Stirling, for Prince James' christening," said Fincastle once the cavalcade was finally ready and they were clattering down Craigmillar Hill, heading north towards Edinburgh. Catching Margaret's eye, he added, "He wants us to take part."

Margaret raised her eyebrows, taking a moment before she replied to settle the mare, who was jogging sideways after spotting a goose rooting through a pile of frost-rimed leaves next to a byre on the outskirts of Pepper Mill village. "He mentioned it to me last night. Are you to play The Bruce again?"

"Nay, I believe he is inspired by mythology this time. Satyrs and the like. There is to be a mechanical chariot. Or ship —I am unsure of the details," he said with a curl of his lip, "and dancing."

"Perhaps I will ask him to do without me this time. My sense of rhythm would embarrass a drunken swine. I am not much of a dancer," Margaret admitted.

"And neither am I." Fincastle gave her a conspiratorial grin. "Shall we sit this one out?"

Margaret grimaced. "I'm not sure we'll be allowed to."

The laird glanced behind him to see if anyone was listening, then leaned closer and said in a whisper, "If we make enough of a bodge of the dancing, he will not want us."

Margaret glanced sideways at him, just in time to catch him winking at her. Despite herself, she laughed at his audacity. "It seems you have it all planned, sire."

"Anything that saves me from prancing around like a three-legged pony. 'Tis not something that should be inflicted on my worst enemy, let alone the dignitaries who will attend the baptism."

"I cannot believe you have enemies, sire," Margaret said without thinking, then berated herself inwardly. He would think she admired him, saying something like that.

But was that not what she wanted him to understand, so she could find out his plans against the queen?

Grey-blue eyes met hers. "You do not wish to know," he said grimly.

The clouds that chased across his countenance silenced her for a moment. "What is it like, living in the Highlands?" she asked, to distract him from the rather dangerous turn their conversation had taken.

"'Tis not so different from the lowlands," he replied, his face clearing. He waved an arm to indicate the pastoral landscape around them, where scruffy sheep snuffled through the frost to reach the grass of the Priest Field. On the left, gorse bushes dotted the rougher ground leading to Kamron, with a burn beside them indicating the route they should follow to the ford ahead. "Just that the hills are higher and the lochs are deeper." He looked at her from under his heavy eyebrows. "Have ye never travelled north?"

"No," she confessed. "The queen went to Aberdeen to deal with the northern rebellion at the Battle of Corrachie four years ago, but 'twas before I became a lady-in-waiting."

"Aberdeen does not really count as the Highlands. Even where I live in Perthshire, 'tis only the edge of the Highlands. But you can see the white peaks of the Cairngorm mountains in the distance, with deer and golden eagle as common as sheep and cattle are down here," he said, pointing at a ewe who was pawing determinedly at the thin cap of ice that had formed over a drinking pool where the stream flowed through her field. "And in summer the heather glows purple like the cloak of a queen, the gorse flowers yellow as the gold of a crown, and the sky is so wide you can surely see the whole of creation. 'Tis truly God's own country."

"You make it sound magnificent. But is it not true that the people run around naked with only a scrap of fabric tied around them, and that some of them have tails?"

This made him laugh out loud. "'Tis the English who have tails, my lady, or so I'm told. But the gentlefolk of the Highlands are but canny and thrifty. If the ground is wet, they will go barefoot to save their boots. And if they cannot afford a coat they use a length of tight-woven woollen cloth to protect them from the weather or to wrap around them as a blanket for sleeping. 'Tis merely practical, not fantastical."

Margaret was silent for a moment, concentrating on directing her mare over the slippery stones underfoot as they splashed across the Black Ford. The stream flowed silently under overhanging trees, and in the sheltered spots a sheen of silver fringed the edges of the watercourse. She pulled her cape more tightly around her shoulders.

"And what is it like, where you are from, Lady Carwood?" Fincastle asked.

For a moment, Margaret considered giving him at evasive answer. But then she remembered that she was trying to win his trust, and pursed her lips. "My parents owned Carwood House, near Biggar—a good number of miles south and west of here. But when they died…" she looked down at her hands. "'Tis a long story. A story that ends with my poor sister married to a man I hate, and me in the queen's service." She tilted her chin and looked him in the eye. "But I am very happy here. Her Grace treats me well, and I want for nothing."

~

Bothwell spurred his horse to catch up with the queen at the head of the cavalcade. "You wanted to speak with me, Your Grace?"

"Oui. Come closer, my lord." Mary motioned for him to come alongside her white palfrey. On her other side jogged Bastian Pages, her valet, and just behind rode Mary Seton and Mary Beaton, her chief ladies-in-waiting.

Bothwell moved his horse until he rode stirrup to stirrup with the queen. "Is there something I can do for you, ma'am?"

"Oui," Mary said again. "I have been talking with Bastian here about the christening celebrations at Stirling. He is taking charge of the entertainments on the final day. There is going to be a three-day pageant like those I remember from my youth in France. But nothing like this has ever been seen in Scotland before, and it is a huge undertaking. I wondered if you could help me by organising the hunt?"

"But of course, ma'am." If Bothwell hadn't been riding, he'd have rubbed his hands together in glee. The queen had chosen *him*, of all her nobles, to assist with the baptism festival.

The queen inclined her head. "Merci. You can meet with the head forester when we reach Stirling. We shall hunt on Wednesday morn, the day after the baptism, and I am expecting a large number of guests from England and France. So make sure he has the woods well stocked."

"Of course, ma'am. And if I may suggest something," he tilted his head at her, "mayhap we could organise a smaller hunt on the afternoon of Monday, to entertain those who arrive early?"

"D'accord. But use a different park for that. Perhaps Saint Ninians. The forester will know where the best sport is to be had. But I shall not attend—I should stay in the castle to greet the ambassadors. Now, the other thing," she turned in her saddle and beckoned to Mary Seton, "Lady Seton is organising new outfits for the king and I, my brother, Moray, and my sister the countess of Argyll. I would like for you to have one too. You can choose from green, blue or red cloth."

Bothwell's chest swelled with pride. The queen was choosing to clothe him the same as her half-brother and half-sister. Did that mean she was thinking of him as royalty? "Blue, ma'am, if it please you. And I am greatly honoured by your consideration."

"Bon. Lady Seton will make arrangements with you when we reach Holyrood."

Bastian rode off somewhere to make more arrangements about the baptismal masque, and the Maries were gossiping about some court tattle, which left Bothwell to accompany the queen. He rode beside her with his head high and his spirits buoyant. Did the commoners who lined the streets think he was the king? He smiled at the thought.

One day he might be.

He had a plan, and it was working. Perhaps at Stirling the next link in the chain would fall into place.

Meeting Margaret's gaze, John kept his face expressionless, showing no sign of what he was *really* thinking. Outwardly, he drew his mouth into a sympathetic line. Inwardly, he grinned in triumph, as if he had turned a corner and spied the centre of a tricky maze.

For Margaret's words had given him some insight into her prickly character, and helped to explain her independent spirit. "We have the whole journey," he lifted a hand off the reins to indicate their route ahead, "so there is more than ample time for a long story. And," he shrugged, "you would be doing me a service. 'Tis a cold morning and a long ride to the palace. A good tale would while away the time."

"I know not that it is *good*, sire. 'Tis a sad and sorry story of betrayal and loss."

He looked sideways at her. "Nevertheless, it will take my mind off the pease porridge I ate for breakfast that churns around in my stomach like a chemise on washday, and the lump in Dirk's saddle," he rolled his eyes, "that rubs a bigger blister on my behind with every mile that we travel."

This last comment made her laugh out loud. "My lord, you are wasted in the Highlands. You should surely be writing your own masques when you can turn a phrase so eloquently."

John was about to reply when there was a

shout of, "Bonjour!" accompanied by the clatter of trotting hooves.

Seconds later, Bastian Pages drew his spritely grey alongside. "Laird Fincastle," the Frenchman inclined his head at John, "and my Lady Carwood. May I take a moment of your time this fine morning?"

Clenching his teeth to stop his face from showing his feelings, John suppressed a sigh, for with this interruption he would not get to hear Margaret's story, and next time they spoke her usual waspish nature would likely have returned and she would refuse to open up.

Margaret, however, greeted the queen's Master of Ceremonies quite cordially. "Of course, sire," she said with a gracious sweep of her gloved hand. "Do join us. Although," she looked around her at the bare trees and the grey air and gave a mock shiver, "I think we need to get you eyeglasses. For I would not call this frigid morning 'fine'. We are at least four months away from any weather I am likely to reckon as good."

Bastian gave a wry smile. "You are right, my lady. I am just happy today. The queen has agreed that Christina and I can marry in February—on the ninth."

The ninth. Just over two months away, and week before John's deadline. He didn't have long to fulfil the terms of the inheritance, and ice swirled in his stomach. *I will need to do it soon.*

"Of course you will both come?" Bastian's sharp eyes glanced from Margaret to John. "There will be a feast. And dancing."

At the mention of dancing, John caught Margaret's eye and surreptitiously raised an eyebrow. "Well, if there is to be dancing," he said to Bastian, "I think you will find that my gavotte will give great entertainment to your guests." He winked at Margaret, then inclined his head. "Thank ye for the invitation."

Margaret's cheeks dimpled with a suppressed smile as she formed her reply. "Monsieur Pages, I would be honoured to celebrate with you and Christina. 'Tis good news that you have a date for your wedding! And no surprise that you are happy."

Up ahead, the cavalcade had slowed to pass through the turnpike gate at Gibbet-Toll on the outskirts of Edinburgh.

At one side of the road, the baillie's children gawked at the fine lords and ladies passing by, their faces glowing red, probably from a scrub in the trough to honour the queen.

On the other side stood the dolorous gatekeeper himself, puffing solemnly on a pipe and eyeing everyone that passed as if measuring them for the scaffold. Next to him stood his wife, dressed in her best green gown over a kirtle made from country russet, cheeks flushed and fingers twining nervously in the ribbons of her bodice.

Bastian pushed his horse ahead, leaving

John and Margaret to pass through the gate in double file. As they rode by, John took his eyes off the road to nod at the baillie, and in that same moment, one of the more enterprising boys pulled the cap off his head, bowed low and held out a hand, entreating, "Spare a penny, m'lord?"

The child's sudden movement and the wave of his hat through the air like a flag spooked Margaret's horse, who skittered sideways and almost knocked the Baillie's wife over. Her yelp of fright unsettled the chestnut mare further.

One glance at Margaret's face was enough to convince John to push Dirk closer alongside, using the gelding's bulk and phlegmatic character to help calm the fractious mare. To distract Margaret, who looked almost as tense as her horse, John asked, "How far is it to Holyrood? Are we nearly there?"

"'Tis a mile or two. We should get there

soon." She clenched her jaw and narrowed her eyes at the mare. "If I get there at all. This one feels like she has stepped on an anthill."

"Aye. Mayhap she needs a good run. That would take the wind out of her sails. Could we take her for a gallop somewhere? Maybe in the queen's park?" John flicked his eyes to the right, where the bulky lump of Arthur's Seat dominated the landscape in the royal hunting grounds.

Margaret grimaced. "I cannot. The queen must lead the procession, and her court must follow. She will go no faster than a walk until we reach the palace, so as to give her people time to see their ruler and her lords and ladies." She lifted her shoulders. "And with this large a company, 'twill be a slow ride. 'Tis the way of it."

"Ah." *How else can I distract her?* John wracked his brains. "And when we leave for Stirling on Monday, will we travel via the village of Queen's Ferry?" The little village on the coast where the pious Queen Margaret had established a ferry to carry pilgrims travelling to St Andrews in Fife was a pretty spot that John had travelled through on his way south from Perthshire.

"No, that is the longer route. We go via Gogar and Kirkliston, and will stop overnight at Linlithgow."

Ember had quieted somewhat now, and John gave Dirk a pat on the neck when the gelding pushed his nose towards the mare, as if to tell her that everything was alright. Margaret seemed less apprehensive too. *My strategy is working.*

By this time the road had widened, and Bastian joined them again. "Laird Fincastle, Lady Carwood," he addressed them, "the other reason I came to speak to you was to ask if you would help me with the christening entertainments."

Margaret tilted her head at the Frenchman. "But of course, sire, did we not already agree to take part?"

"Oui, but I need you to do something different. I am preparing the programme for the baptismal feast on the third day. But now the queen has decided that she wants a pageant on the green outside the castle in the afternoon to—eh—*distract* her guests while the servants prepare for the investiture in the evening. I am so busy designing the stage for the dinner—would you be able to take charge of the afternoon performance? Her Grace wants something that will represent the strength of a God-given monarchy against the forces of the world." Bastian spoke so enthusiastically his words almost tripped over themselves like leaves chased by an autumn gale. "You can use soldiers from her honour guard if you need additional performers. And at the end of the afternoon the queen has commissioned a firework display which will end your masque."

John and Margaret exchanged a look. John was first to speak. "Sire, I am truly honoured that you would ask us—but surely there is one amongst the nobles who would be better qualified than Lady Carwood or me?"

"I think not." Bastian inclined his head at each of them in turn. "You are both experienced players, with a sense of the dramatic. I am sure you will not let me down. Now," he tightened his hands on the reins, "I must go and speak to the head armourer. Au revoir, mes amis." Turning his horse's head, he trotted away, leaving John and Margaret open-mouthed in his wake.

"I fear this is your fault, my lady," said John. "Did you not say that I should be writing a play? It seems your prophecy will come true."

Margaret gave him a rueful smile. "I may live to regret that."

"Aye. You and me both."

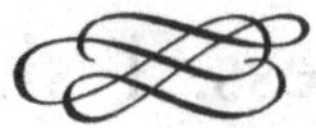

CHAPTER 4

The closer they got to Holyrood Palace, the more people that lined the streets to cheer—or gawp—at the royal procession. And the more people that crowded on either side of her, the more agitated Margaret's horse became.

By the time they were clattering along the final stretches of the busy road that led to the royal palace, Ember was jogging sideways and frothing at the bit. "I thought the journey would settle her, but—" Margaret gasped as the mare caught sight of a serge-clad goodwife with a heavy creel of fish strapped to her back, and leapt in the air.

John pushed his gelding closer. "Not far now."

"Thank goodness. I shall have no teeth left. I think she's rattled them all out of my head."

"The crowds unsettle her, I think."

"My lord, you are a master of understatement." Margaret risked a quick glimpse at the Highlander. The breadth of his smile and the benign look on his face seemed to indicate that her plan to win his confidence was working. Surely she would soon be able to get to the bottom of whatever intrigue he and the other lords were plotting, and ensure the queen was kept safe?

When the iron gates of the palace hove into sight, Margaret breathed a sigh of relief. *Nearly there.* "I'll ask for a different horse for the ride to Stirling," she said to nobody in particular.

The laird caught his breath to reply, then covered his mouth as a torrent of coughs wracked his chest. "Excuse me," he said when he'd recovered, "the smoke in the air plays havoc with my lungs."

Margaret quirked her brow at him.

He shrugged, his face unreadable. "I… got too close to a fire, once."

Methinks there is a story there. But there was not enough time to hear it. Ahead of them, the royal party disappeared into the palace courtyard, while some of the guards peeled off through the gate into Holyrood Park and their barracks behind the palace. In the wan light of the winter afternoon, the grassy flanks of Arthur's Seat looked grey, and the forbidding crags loomed like brown fangs in the maw of a sleeping giant.

With their destination in sight, Margaret rolled her shoulders and flexed her fingers on the reins.

But she relaxed too soon.

To their left, a brewer's dray turned the corner from Carlton Road, and caught a wheel on something—a stone, the gutter, Margaret never found out what—dislodging one of the casks piled high on its stout boards. The barrel tumbled over the side and clattered to the ground with a noise like the blast of a caliver.

For Margaret's mare, it was like a match to touchpaper. She shot to the side, then turned and aimed towards the gate ahead and the open spaces of the queen's park.

Clinging grimly to the saddle with her knees, Margaret pulled ineffectually at the reins, trying with all her might to stop the horse, or at least to slow her headlong flight. But she had as much effect on the mare as King Canute trying to stop an incoming tide, and within seconds they were galloping across the springy turf of the royal hunting grounds, Ember's neck stretched out like the bowsprit of a galleon and Margaret's cloak flying behind them like a battle standard.

On another occasion, Margaret might have relished a fast ride in picturesque countryside. But enjoyment was usually accompanied by at least a modicum of control, and right then she felt helpless—and embarrassed. The queen gave her this horse because she thought Margaret would manage her, maybe even improve her. Instead, she had let the mare run away, and made her worse! Trees flashed past on Margaret's left, and on her right, a stand of bracken disappeared in a blur of orange.

Setting her teeth, Margaret hauled on the reins again, determined to best the horse. But it was no use—the mare's jaw was rigid, the muscles of her neck set like a wooden board. "Ember," Margaret cried, "you make me look like a novice rider!" With more space, she might have tried to turn her steed in ever-decreasing circles. But this strip of land between the palace and the hill was like a channel, leading to… A chill ran down Margaret's spine.

Saint Margaret's Loch.

And Ember was headed right to it, her ears locked forward like a terrier who had cornered a mouse in a stable.

If she could swim, Margaret might not have worried so much. But she had never learned after the tragedy of her parents' death. *So this is how I die*, she thought, and frantically tried to drag the mare off course, knowing as she did so that she risked pulling the horse off-balance and making her fall. But surely anything would be better than a watery grave?

The green-black waters of the loch loomed ahead, filling Margaret's vision and causing panic to swirl in her chest like a flock of starlings at twilight. With herculean strength, born of desperation, she made one last attempt to pull the mare aside, but to no avail.

Lord save me!

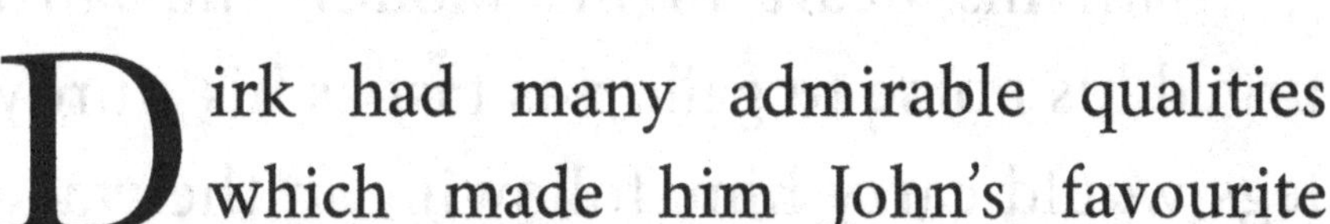

Dirk had many admirable qualities which made him John's favourite mount. But speed wasn't one of them.

Ahead of them, Ember's tail streamed behind her like a ribbon in a hurricane as Margaret fought to regain control, the mare's pounding hooves taking them further and further from the palace and safety, and away from her pursuers.

Back in the procession, as soon as he realised what was happening, John had spun Dirk and chased after Margaret, with sparks flying on the cobbles as Dirk's hooves scrabbled for purchase on the slippery surface. A few seconds later, when they flew through the gates of the park behind Margaret, a couple of mounted soldiers realised that the noblewoman was in trouble, and also joined in the pursuit. But their hobblers had considerably shorter legs than John's hunter, and they trailed even further back.

With his heart in his mouth, the laird urged his horse to gallop as fast as his sturdy legs would carry him, following in the wake of the mare.

Looking over his shoulder, the laird spotted the receding figures of the cavalrymen. "They will be no help. 'Tis up to you and me to save her, Dirk." He crouched lower over the gelding's neck and applied his spurs again. "Give me everything you've got."

The gelding's nostrils flared and his ears flattened as he charged after the runaway. With this extra effort, they were no longer falling behind. *Perhaps the mare tires.* But she was still a good distance ahead, and had almost reached the steep banks of the loch. Surely she would stop before the water?

And stop Ember did, but not until her

front hooves had almost skidded into the loch, halting with such violence that Margaret catapulted over her head, landing with a huge splash in the black waters of the loch.

"Help!" Margaret called out in panic as her heavy skirts spread around her.

The weight will pull her under. But she was only a short distance from the shore. 'Twould not be far for her to swim, even if her clothes were waterlogged. Reining Dirk to a halt, John leapt down and started to pull off his boots, ready to wade in and help Margaret out of the water.

But instead of swimming, Lady Carwood flailed her arms like a windmill and started to disappear beneath the surface.

She cannot swim! John realised, and his insides turned to ice. With renewed speed, he threw off his woollen cloak and velvet doublet, then jumped into the cold water, his eyes fixed on the spot where Margaret had disappeared.

With a couple of strong pulls he reached the spot, took a quick gulp of air then dived down into the murky water, eyes peering through the gloom. It was like a pea soup, and he could see nothing.

With urgency borne of desperation, John swung his gaze left and right, eyes straining to divine the shape of the drowning woman, but there was no sign of her. Diving deeper and reaching out with his arms in case he would feel her rather than seeing her, John cast around until his fingers touched the muddy bottom of the loch. *She is not here.* His heart constricted, even as his lungs started to burn for want of air. But he'd seen her fall in. *I must have the wrong spot.*

With a thrust of his feet he pushed off from the bed of the loch, swimming at an angle and scanning from side to side as he rose through the water in case he passed her. Seconds later he'd reached the surface and was gulping some blessed air, turning this way and that, searching for some sign of her location.

On the banks of the loch, the soldiers had caught up—and caught the disgraced horse. Helmets waving like flags, they jumped up and down like madmen, hollering to catch his attention and pointing at a spot behind him.

He swung around, caught a glimpse of the ripples they'd seen, and before his mind had fully processed it he was diving down again, aiming for this new location. Hands reaching out in front of him as he kicked deeper, he sent up a silent prayer of thanks as he finally touched something solid. *Margaret!*

Placing his arms around her waist, he grasped her tightly, then kicked hard for the surface, hoping against hope that she'd managed to hold her breath, that she wasn't drowned, that somehow she'd survived being submerged in the icy loch. For he'd miss her pretty face and her flaming mane of hair. He'd even miss her waspish tongue and argumentative nature. *Let her be alive,* he prayed, as he reached the surface again and sucked in a huge draught of air.

CHAPTER 5

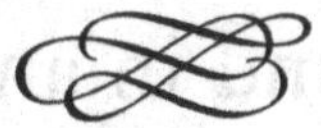

Mary flew down the stairs as fast as was seemly, her heart in her mouth and her mind flying in a hundred directions at once.

At the front door of the palace, a gaggle of servants and courtiers had gathered to greet Laird Fincastle's little cavalcade, who clattered to a halt in the courtyard, horses still blowing hard from their gallop, breath rising like clouds from flaring nostrils.

Atop of Dirk, Margaret and the laird looked like drowned rats, water dripping from their hair, and sodden fabric clinging to their bodies. Margaret swayed drunkenly, and it was surely only the laird's strong arm around her waist that prevented her from falling to the ground in an indecorous heap. Behind them, two mounted soldiers led Lady Carwood's prancing horse, their jaws set and brows furrowed.

A worm of guilt worried its way into Mary's guts. *I should not have made her ride that mare.* But she stifled that thought, and addressed the laird. "What 'appened, Laird Fincastle?" she asked, kneading the black satin of her gown with fingers that seemed not to belong to her body. "What ails Lady Carwood?"

Fincastle's teeth chattered as he replied. "Her horse bolted, Your Grace, then threw Lady Carwood into the loch. She nearly drowned."

The blood drained from Mary's face. *'Tis my fault.* But Mary was the queen, and could not be seen to be doubting her own decisions. She straightened her back, then she beckoned a wide-eyed page. "Fetch Doctor Nau and send 'im to my rooms," she instructed. "Quickly!" she added, shooing him away, for the dramatic scene before them seemed to have added lead weights to the boy's feet.

Then she pointed at a couple of footmen. "Get Lady Carwood inside quickly, before she catches a chill," she urged. "Take her to my chamber—the doctor will attend her there."

Handing Margaret down to waiting arms, the laird watched anxiously as she was carried away, his lips flattened and his shoulders tight. Once her bearers had disappeared up the flagstone stairs of the tower, he swung his leg over the horse's rump and dismounted, then handed the reins to a stable hand. "Give him a good rub down and some extra oats tonight," he instructed.

"My lord," Mary called him over, "you need to get inside and get dry too. I shall send a servant to bank the fire in your room." She inclined her head. "My thanks to you for rescuing Lady Carwood. She is my favourite chamberwoman and I would have hated for anything to happen to her."

Fincastle gave a weary bow. "I am only thankful I was able to reach her in time," he said. "I hope she suffers no ill-effects."

Mary indicated for him to walk alongside her, and led the way back into the palace. "Nevertheless," she spoke quietly, for his ears only, "you have done me a great service. Is there any favour I can offer you in return?" She glanced sideways at him. "I hear there is some issue with your inheritance?"

Rubbing his neck, Fincastle paused before answering. "Aye, ma'am, you hear right. I must marry, or I will lose my father's lands in favour of my uncle."

"And do you have a lady in mind?"

Another pause. "There is no-one who will have me, I fear, and time runs out."

But if Mary's eyes had not deceived her during the masque at Craigmillar, the Highlander *did* have an affinity with one of her ladies—the very one he had just risked his life to save.

She would play matchmaker again, and see if love would find a way. "There is still plenty of time, sire—we are already planning a wedding for February the ninth, so it will be no hardship to organise another ceremony the day after." She tapped the side of her nose. "Leave it with me."

But it was not Margaret who suffered most from her impromptu ducking in the loch.

Next morning, John awoke with his throat on fire and what felt like an anvil resting on his ribs. *Damn my weak chest!* Ever since the fire that had taken Lizzy from him, John's lungs had been susceptible to the vagaries of the Scottish weather. Every winter, without fail, he would get a crushing ague which would leave him bedridden for days.

It took less than a minute for the wheeze that accompanied every breath to persuade Duncan, his manservant, to rush off and fetch the doctor.

"Hot water with honey, lemon and a spoonful of this Salix powder," Monsieur Nau held out a little packet once he'd examined the laird, "four times a day. And warm. Keep him warm."

The Frenchman's dark eyebrows drew together as nutmeg-brown eyes bored into the servant. "Keep the fire burning bright. And bring more pillows so he can lie more upright." Then he turned his attention back to John. "You must stay in your bed until you have stopped coughing and your lungs are clear."

"But—I've to ride to Stirling for the Prince's christening."

Monsieur Nau shook his head. "Mais non. Not if you want to get better, my lord. You have a strong constitution, I'm sure, but this is not the right time of year to travel when you have the grippe."

"But…" John's would-be protest tailed off into a fit of coughing. How would he keep an eye on the plotters if they were in Stirling—as they surely would be—and he was abed in Edinburgh? And how could he keep the queen safe, stuck here in this poky room?

"You see? Keep warm, drink your medicine and I will check on you later," said the doctor, picking up his valise and heading for the door, "and again tomorrow before we leave for Stirling."

I must get better soon, vowed John. He

could not afford to lie there a moment longer than necessary.

~

Margaret rose from the green-embroidered hassock, smoothed the imprint of her knees from her dress, then joined the retinue following the queen out of the impressive stone chapel at Holyrood with its incense-laden air and lofty ceilings. As they processed along the yew-lined flagstone path leading back to the palace, Mary motioned for Margaret to come alongside.

"You had a lucky escape yesterday, mon amie," Mary whispered. "And I said many prayers of thanks for you this morning." Margaret was speared by a pair emerald-green eyes. "But I hear your rescuer was not so lucky. Monsieur Nau tells me that Laird Fincastle has the grippe, and is confined to bed."

"Oh!" Memories of yesterday's near-drowning flooded Margaret's mind—murky waters closing around her; strong hands pulling her upwards; someone pushing on her chest until water spewed out of her mouth and she dissolved into a fit of coughing; the feeling of safety atop the big black horse as they returned to the palace. "I should go and thank him."

"I think he deserves more than your thanks."

Margaret looked askance at the queen. *What is she thinking!* Surely the queen would not…

"I want you to stay and nurse him until he is well enough to travel to Stirling," Mary continued.

Oh! Margaret's initial feeling of relief that the queen merely wanted her to perform nursemaid duties was quickly replaced by worry, then annoyance at the idea of being forced to look after the… *miscreant* who was plotting against her mistress. Taking a deep breath, she pushed her anger aside. "But who will look after you and keep you safe if I am left here, ma'am?"

That earned her a sharp glance. "I shall 'ave Lord Bothwell to protect me, and two hundred of his finest soldiers."

"But what about your food, checking it is —unadulterated." Margaret dropped her voice for those last words, for it was not commonly known at court that the queen suspected she had been poisoned a few weeks previously when staying in Jedburgh.

"I shall get one of my pages to taste things first—there is a new cook at Stirling so I have every reason to do so." Mary laid a hand on her handmaid's arm. "I can manage without you for a few days, dear Margaret. Do not concern yourself."

Margaret chewed her lip. The queen didn't know about the plot. Should she tell her so she could be on guard? But Margaret had no proof, and without proof Mary would never suspect her favourite, the Earl of Bothwell.

Perhaps nursemaiding would give her a chance to glean information from Fincastle. Mayhap it was not such a bad idea after all. "As you wish, ma'am."

"Bon! Now…" Mary gave her a sideways look, "Bastian tells me you and the laird are devising the pageant for the afternoon of my son's christening." Her mouth curled up at the side. "I am greatly excited to see what you come up with!"

CHAPTER 6

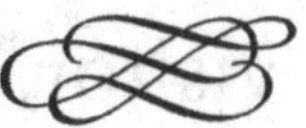

SUNDAY 8TH DECEMBER 1566

A rap on John's bed-chamber door awoke him from a fitful sleep. Blinking in the thin light which filtered around the heavy window-drapes, he levered himself onto an elbow, and immediately dissolved into a paroxysm of coughing.

Duncan, who'd been dozing on a wooden stool beside the fire, rushed to the bedside, his pepper-and-salt eyebrows crunched together and his droopy moustache emphasising the downward curl of his mouth.

Unable to speak until his lungs quieted,

John shooed his manservant away, and indicated for him to let the visitor in.

With a frown, Duncan turned for the door. "I'll fetch a lemon infusion for ye, sire. And tea for yer visitor," he added as he turned the handle to admit whoever was calling.

Convulsions finally over, John lay back on the pillows with his eyes closed, breathing heavily and ignoring his caller. 'Twas probably the doctor, come to prod and powder him some more.

The cool draft from the hall beyond brought with it a rustle of satin, which alerted John that his visitor was not, in fact, the doctor. He opened one heavy eyelid to see a comely woman silhouetted against the light from the open door.

"The queen sent me," said Margaret, settling herself primly on the oak chair beside his bed. "She says I must look after you since you got sick from rescuing me from the loch." She paused, seeming to realise how ungrateful that sounded. "Ah—and I want to offer you my heartfelt thanks for your service, sire. I cannot swim—"

"So I realised," interrupted John, his voice almost a whisper due to the roughness in his throat.

She looked down at her hands. "—I never learned. Not after…"

John's interest was piqued. "Not after…?" he prompted.

Her lips twisted, then she sat taller and glanced at him from under her eyebrows. "'Twas not the done thing, in the Borders. I never learned," she re-iterated.

If he hadn't been so weary, he'd have sighed. *What is she not telling me?* On the way to Holyrood she'd started to tell him a story about her family, but they'd been interrupted by Bastian before he could get her to open up. He would hear that story, he determined, sometime soon. But Margaret was obviously touchy on the subject, so he would need to choose his moment. "When the weather is better I could teach you to swim," he offered, laying a hand on her arm. "If you would like. But 'tis too cold right now."

She stiffened. "I—I thank you. But no, sire. I'm too scared of the water."

And nearly drowning won't have helped. He shrugged, but the movement set off a tickle in his throat and he spent the next minute coughing into his hand. "If you change your mind," he wheezed, hoping she wouldn't notice that his eyes were watering, "the offer stands."

Reaching into a pocket in her dress, Margaret pulled out a leather-bound book. "I thought I could read to you. Since you're ill. You can lie back and rest your lungs." She opened the volume and smoothed its vellum pages. "Boece's *History of Scotland*." Giving him a sideways look, she added, "I thought we could read about your ancestor."

John caught her eye, wondering if she was teasing him. "The Bruce?"

"Yes, The Bruce. We can see if Bastian's masque was based on truth."

~

An hour later, they had established that Bastian had taken some artistic liberties with his masque about King Robert I of Scotland, but that the essence of the story he'd told was true. Robert the Bruce was an ambitious and bold warrior who'd defeated a stronger English army to secure the future of his people as an independent nation. He'd also ensured that his lineage would be their rulers; Queen Mary being the latest of his descendants to hold the throne.

"Her Grace must be a cousin of yours, sire?" Margaret closed the book and raised an eyebrow. Even though she was here only because the queen had ordered, the afternoon had passed quickly and the High-lander's company had not been as irksome as she'd feared, despite his frequent bouts of coughing.

"Aye, distantly. Ninth cousins thirteen times removed or somesuch," he said, rolling his eyes so hard it made her laugh. "My old nan," he paused to catch his breath, chest heaving, "would have been able to tell you chapter and verse, God rest her soul."

"Could we use Bruce's story again in the masque for the baptism? What was it Bastian said? 'Represent the strength of the God-given monarch against the forces of the world'?"

"I think not, my lady." He waved a hand at his long legs under the bedcovers. "Our modern Bruce is somewhat indisposed." As if to illustrate the point, a fit of coughing dou-bled him up for at least a minute.

Margaret summoned Duncan from his

seat at the fireside and requested another hot drink for the invalid.

Once the servant was dispatched, she addressed the laird once more. "We have the Queen's honour guard at our disposal. Perhaps we could use them for the masque, and we ourselves could direct proceedings, rather than acting." She tilted her head. "That might be prudent since we will be delayed in our arrival, and it will be difficult to rehearse."

"Aye. But neither will the soldiers have much time to rehearse."

She pursed her lips. "So we make it easy for them. Utilise what they know already. Drills, sword fights, marching," she waved a hand airily, "soldierly things."

"Mayhap I should organise that part?" he answered with a lift of an eyebrow, voice rasping like a lock that needed oil.

She snorted. *He has a way of making me laugh,* she thought. But he looked tired. It seemed this had been too much for him. "Mayhap. But for now I think you need quiet. Your cough is getting worse."

"But the masque—"

"We can arrange that on the morrow. Or the day after. 'Tis eleven days till the Prince's investiture. It can wait."

Duncan reappeared, holding two steaming goblets in front of him as he opened the door using his shoulder and a leather-booted foot. "I brung one for you too, ma'am," he said, laying the drinks on the maplewood cabinet beside Fincastle's bed. "And a twist o' the medicine the doctor prescribed for Laird Fincastle."

"Thank you," she said, then sprinkled the salix powder into the Highlander's drink and handed it to him.

Her own infusion, when she supped it, was more tasty than she'd expected. "Honey and lemon," she sniffed at the steam rising off the top of the liquid, "and a hint of something spicy perhaps?" she asked the manservant.

"Aye, ma'am, Cook adds some ginger as well."

She smiled. "'Tis tasty. Now," she addressed the laird, "sit forward a moment till I fix the bolster behind your back."

Pillows adjusted, Fincastle lay back, his eyelids drooping.

Carefully, she took the goblet from his hand and placed it on the cabinet alongside her own.

The laird's strong features softened and his breathing eased as he drifted off to sleep, making his handsome face look almost boyish.

Who would think he was a rogue, plotting against the queen? Suppressing a sigh, Margaret adjusted the woollen blanket covering his bed, and tucked it up under his armpits. *'Tis always the ones you'd least expect.*

"Thank ye, my dear." Whispered so softly

she almost missed it, Fincastle smiled and laid a hand on hers, his eyes still closed.

Even as she froze at his touch, something about the warmth of his skin or the intimacy of being in his bedchamber, made Margaret's cheeks flush and her heart thump. *He probably mistook me for his wife. His dead wife,* she told herself, breathing slowly in an effort to control her pulse.

A minute later, when she was sure her complexion was back to normal and the laird was properly asleep, Margaret slipped her hand from under his and stood up.

On the other side of the room, Duncan eyed her speculatively, smoothing his moustache between finger and thumb.

Giving him her most withering look, Margaret stuck her nose in the air and left the room quickly, before her cheeks would colour again and give the manservant even more to gossip about in the servants' quarters.

Feet pattering on the stone floor, she hurried up the turnpike stair to her room, shoulders drooping more with every step.

The next few days would be challenging. She must nurse a man she ought to despise, yet found strangely compelling. It would test all her resolve. But her loyalty to the queen would sustain her, she was sure. Clenching her fist, she dug her fingernails into the palm. *It must.*

Hooves clattered on the stony ground and echoed on the outer walls of Linlithgow Palace as the queen and her retinue left their overnight stop, bound for Stirling. It was a grey morning, but Bothwell's mood was light as he slotted into his place at Mary's right-hand side.

It was becoming expected, now, his

riding with the queen. Especially in the absence of her husband.

Thanks to his unswerving loyalty to both her and her mother before her, she seemed to trust him, and had even started asking him for advice rather than listening to her secretary, Maitland. It was a situation he relished, and one that he intended to take *full* advantage of.

At the side of the road, some of the local women had gathered to watch the spectacle, dressed in homespun wool and rough linen, faces awestruck at the sight of the nobility in their feathers and finery. Some of the women waved handkerchiefs and cheered as the cavalcade passed.

Bothwell was not a fanciful man, but riding alongside the monarch at the head of the members of court, he could imagine what it must feel like to be king. Puffing out his chest, he pulled a handful of farthings from his pocket, and tossed them magnanimously at some young boys in tattered shirts who were running alongside the procession.

Let them think he was the king. If his plans came to fruition, he *would* be, someday soon. Then his face clouded.

"What ails you, my lord Bothwell?" The queen spoke from the side of her mouth even as she smiled and waved at her subjects.

"'Tis naught," Bothwell dissembled. But the thought of his plans had brought to mind the Highland limmer who'd muscled his way into their plot against the king. Could he *really* be trusted? He had not come to Linlithgow with them—Bothwell had examined every face at dinner last evening. Was he even now riding to tell the king, or pulling together a counter-plot?

The earl gripped his reins tighter, making his horse jog nervously, then turned to the queen. "But I wondered if you have seen Laird Fincastle? I need to speak to him about," he thought quickly, "a ram I wish to purchase."

"Oh, he has the grippe," Mary said airily as she steadied her horse to guide him through the West Port. "He is recovering at Holyrood and will join us at Stirling later."

But her words did not assuage Bothwell. The Highlander could have used illness as a cover for treachery, and could even now be conniving against them. If he was, the earl would kill him, he surely would. Blow him up with his own gunpowder if he had to.

Bothwell smiled. There would be some vindication in that.

~

It was three days before they were able to discuss the masque again.

In the intervening time, the queen and her retinue had left for Stirling Castle, where the young Prince's baptism was to take place.

After a night in Linlithgow Palace to break the journey, they had arrived safely, and preparations for the christening festivities had entered their 'final, fervid, stages', according to a hurried missive Margaret had received from Bastian.

Normally, Margaret would have suspected the Frenchman of exaggeration, knowing his love of drama. But since her mistress was in equal parts determined and paranoid about this important event going off without a hitch, it was possible that, for once, Bastian was actually under-playing how frenetic things were at court.

Placing the letter under a bronze paper-weight on her writing-table, Margaret suffered a twinge of guilt. *I should be there.*

The queen needed her—relied on her, even, now that Mary Beaton and Mary Livingston were married and spending more time with their husbands than at court. With Mary Fleming also busy, engaged as she was to the queen's secretary, William Maitland, it only left the chaste Mary Seton in support of the monarch.

But what Margaret did here was important too. Nursing the Highlander was what her mistress had ordered, and it allowed her to get closer to the laird. If God was on her side, that would enable her to unmask the plot once Fincastle re-joined the rest of his conspirators in Stirling.

Unfortunately, the laird was not yet well enough to travel. In fact, he'd been worse for the last few days; sweating and feverish, and coughing constantly. His throat was so raw he could hardly speak above a whisper.

With a sigh, Margaret smoothed her skirt, then picked up her book and headed for the stairs. 'Twas time to visit with the Highlander.

Entering Fincastle's chamber, Margaret blinked. The heavy drapes had been drawn back, allowing weak sunlight to filter into the room which illuminated dust motes in front of the window and cobwebs in the corners. *I shall need to send a maid,* Margaret thought, then turned her attention to the laird. "Good morning, sire."

"Good morning, Margaret," croaked the Highlander, his voice weak, but considerably stronger than it had been yesterday. His complexion looked better too, and he was sitting up in bed, rather than languishing under the covers. She wrinkled her nose. *One thing is worse though.*

"Duncan, does your master have a clean chemise? Methinks we need to change him out of the sweaty thing he's been wearing these last days."

"Aye ma'am." Rooting around in a cedarwood chest, Duncan produced a pristine linen shirt.

It was only once they had the laird half-way out of his dirty undergarment that Margaret realised the folly of her actions. She'd been so intent on improving the air in Fincastle's room that she hadn't thought about the fact that he'd end up half-naked. *I should've called for a servant to help,* she thought, as Duncan pulled the chemise over his master's head, revealing shoulders so strong they reminded her of an ox, and a muscular chest so impressive that it stopped the breath in her throat.

Dragging her gaze away, she swallowed hard, trying vainly to regain her composure. *I will burn in hell for this.*

Grabbing the dirty shirt from the manservant, she rushed to the door and dropped it in the corridor outside, ready for a laundry maid to collect. "That should make you more comfortable," she said as she turned back into the room, hardly daring to lift her eyes.

But Duncan had spared her blushes, and already had the Highlander clothed in the fresh shirt. His own face, however, wore that knowing smirk again, even as he fussed over the lacing at the open neck of his master's chemise.

Ignoring the servant, which was her only option apart from fleeing again, she seated herself at Fincastle's bedside and folded her hands atop her book. "'Tis good you seem more recovered, sire. Do you feel well enough to talk about our plans for the masque?"

"Aye." He lifted his chin to call his servant over. "But a drink would make my throat easier. Shall I get Duncan to fetch ye some o' cook's lemon and ginger too?"

She inclined her head. "Thank you. Yes."

A moment later, Duncan was dispatched, and the laird lowered his voice. "I'm sorry if ye were discomfited earlier."

Margaret waved a hand. "'Twas nothing. I —I'm not used to such things. If I hadn't been in such a hurry to make you more comfortable I'd have thought to call a servant to help."

"Well, I thank ye for your kindness." The corners of his eyes crinkled. "And I've been thinking about the masque, what you said about letting the soldiers be soldiers, and what Bastian said about showing the strength of our God-given monarch against the forces of the world." He smoothed the woven blanket that covered his bed. "How would it be if we—you, or I—represent the Stuart line—the prince, the queen—and the soldiers attack us, again and again, in different guises, playing the different armies that have attacked the crown over the years. And we win." He lifted an eyebrow. "Of course."

Fincastle's words sparked a memory, and a series of images flashed through Margaret's mind: a horde attacking, weapons bristling, faces fierce. Somewhere, a fire burned, the acrid smoke tickling her nostrils and stinging her eyes, causing tears to flow down her cheeks. Or was she weeping from fear?

All she remembered of that terrible night —apart from the distressing sight of lawless reivers attacking Carwood House—was how frightened she felt, how worried she'd been for mother and father, and how relieved she'd been when the attackers had finally been repelled...

A hand on her arm startled her from her childhood recollection. "Margaret," the laird's voice was soft, "I'm sorry. 'Twas a ridiculous idea." He touched a finger to his forehead. "My fever affected my imagination."

"No, no." She shook her head, trying to dispel the disturbing pictures. "'Tis a good idea. 'Twould be dramatic. And easy for the soldiers. We could have them attack a castle." A picture of her home, walls scorched by smoke and pockmarked by bullet holes, swam unbidden into her head. She thrust the memory away. "Or a palace. To make it obvious who we are."

"Or we could wear a crown? Crowns," he corrected himself.

"That too!" In Margaret's vision she now wore a cloak and crown, and when she raised the royal sceptre, the reivers fell to the ground as if dead. She smiled grimly. "We can show the might of the throne of Scotland. Her Grace will love this!"

"And it should be easy for the soldiers to rehearse." The laird seemed relieved that she liked his idea, his eagerness to please making him seem younger, somehow, smoothing the lines from his face and brightening skin made pallid by his sickness.

Perhaps if she could get even closer to him, he would want to please her and she could get him to share the details of the plot against the queen? But she could not countenance getting intimate with him. No matter how handsome he might be. *My soul would burn in hell.* There had to be another way.

"Yes. But first, let us work on the order of battle, so we can send instructions to Stirling." Opening the history book she held, she pulled her chair closer to the Highlander's bed, so that he could see the pages too. It meant that her arm now lay against his bicep. *But that cannot be helped,* she thought, even as her breathing quickened at his touch. "This book should tell us of Scotland's enemies."

"Ah." Fincastle cleared his throat, glanced at her briefly, then tapped a finger pensively against his blanket.

In the silence that ensued, Duncan reappeared and handed them both a warm drink.

"Sire?" she enquired when the laird had not spoken for at least a minute.

"'Tis just—" he gave her a pained look, "Scotland's worst enemy has always been the English. And will the English queen not be a guest at the christening? We would not want to offend her."

"She has been invited. But she will not come. Some say she is scared to meet her cousin, in case our queen is more beautiful than she." Margaret pursed her lips. "But she will send some of her nobles, and those popinjays can be more easily offended than Elizabeth herself."

"So we should not have the English attacking."

"No. And we need to make it obvious the attackers *aren't* English, lest they take offence wrongly."

John stared at Margaret's book for a moment. "Mayhap we could represent those who've been enemies of both England and Scotland? Like the norsemen, with their helmets and longboats, or the barbarians during the Crusades?"

"Yes! And we could show that she reigns

by God's will by having devilish hordes at-tack as well. And be defeated."

John nodded slowly. "Aye. Three waves of attackers should be enough. They will get the point, without getting bored."

Sitting taller, Margaret pulled the book back onto her lap, and folded her hands primly atop it. "So we have a plan. I shall send word to Stirling."

"Duncan!" The laird called his manser-vant over. "Find us some writing paper and a pen so we can write instructions for the cap-tain of the guard."

Moments later, Duncan had disappeared again in search of writing implements and they were left alone; the only sound the crackling of the open fire on the far wall.

"My lady." Margaret almost jumped out of her chair as a warm hand was laid on her arm. "I just wanted to say," continued the High-lander, his voice rich and warm like spiced wine, "how much I have appreciated your company these last days." Blue eyes like deep pools pulled her in so she felt she was drowning in his presence. She couldn't look away. "The hours have passed faster—and more pleasantly—with you here. I hope we can continue our friendship even once the masque is over."

For possibly the first time in her adult life, Margaret was lost for words. Or more rightly, the words refused to come, as she was held by his gaze, mesmerised by the beauty of him. Somehow, her hand found its way to his arm, but the warmth of it broke the spell he had woven around her. *He is a magician.*

Sliding her hand back onto her lap, she cleared her throat. "Ah, yes, if you are staying at court, no doubt we will encounter one another."

But she would need to keep her distance. Being as close to him as this was not good for her health. Or her resolve.

CHAPTER 7

FRIDAY 13TH DECEMBER 1566

With a last look at the grey skies outside, John whirled away from the window and grabbed a cloak from a peg in the corner, pulling it around his shoulders. "I am going to the stables," he announced to Duncan, who sat on his usual stool by the fire. "I must check on Dirk, lest they are letting him get lazy."

"But sire—" The laird never heard the rest of Duncan's objection, as it was cut short by the timbers of the heavy oak door thumping closed behind him. He smiled grimly. Duncan was a good manservant, but sometimes he worried too much.

And in truth John's concern about Dirk was merely an excuse. In reality, the laird was being driven mad by being cooped up in that small room—even if his days were made brighter by the visits of the queen's handmaid—and he needed to get outside, go somewhere, do *something*, to remind his legs of their function and blow the stench of sickness from his hair. 'Twas two days now since his fever had broken and he felt better—still weak as a kitten, evidenced by how often he had to stop to catch his breath on his way to the stables—but considerably better than he'd been a few days ago.

His spirits revived even more when he entered the stables and found Margaret already there, her fiery locks sparkling in the flickering lamp-light inside the stone building. She was deep in discussion with the head ostler, and didn't notice John's approach until he coughed politely.

"Sire!" she exclaimed, her face turning pink. "You are out of your bed!" She swallowed, the blush rising up her cheeks. "Evidently."

'Twas interesting to see her discomfited, and he suppressed a smile. "Aye." He inclined his head. "I'd had enough of the sick room to last a lifetime. Thought I'd come and see Dirk." Then his eyes lit on the horses behind her, and the large packs stowed behind their saddles. He frowned. "Going somewhere?"

Her face flushed properly crimson. "To Linlithgow." Her eyes lowered. "And then Stirling," she added, almost in a whisper.

An arrow speared through John's heart. "On your own?"

"That is what I was discussing with the groom. Whether he could spare a man to ride with me." She glanced up at him, pupils dark and irises grey in the low light. "I know the queen asked me to take care of you, but the weather is turning and I thought if I could get to Stirling before it breaks I can organise the masque, and leave you here to recuperate properly..."

Conflicting emotions surged in John's breast. Admiration for her bravery and independence warred with concern for her safety, should she take to the roads on her own. The lowlands of Scotland during Mary's reign were relatively safe, but that did not mean that robbers or worse might not take advantage of a lonely traveller. Especially a woman, who would always be more vulnerable.

"'Tis good, then, that I am recovered," he said, hoping his voice sounded stronger than he felt. Surely this ague could not affect him for much longer? He could recuperate further on the journey—Dirk was so comfortable to ride it was almost like sitting on an old armchair.

He turned to the stable-hand. "See to it, please, that my horse is also made ready for the journey, and Duncan's beast, Bracken."

"Sire, there is no need. I will be fine on my own," Margaret protested, tilting her chin upwards. But the rapid rise and fall of her partlet provided evidence that she was not as calm as she outwardly appeared.

John caught her gaze. "Even so, I would never forgive myself if anything happened to you. And the queen would make garters from my guts if you met any danger. Duncan and I will be your companions." He looked over her shoulder. "Have you found a new horse? Not that Ember?"

Suppressing a smile, she shook her head. "Not Ember. Never again!" Her eyes flashed. "They have found a nice steady gelding for me."

"Good." He turned to the ostler. "Have the horses ready in fifteen minutes."

Margaret gave him a sideways look, her

brow creasing. "Have you had breakfast, sire? I did not see you in the dining hall."

He lifted a shoulder. "I am not—"

"Nonsense!" That sharp tongue was back in evidence again as she over-rode him. "An hour," she told the groom, "and then we will leave for Stirling!"

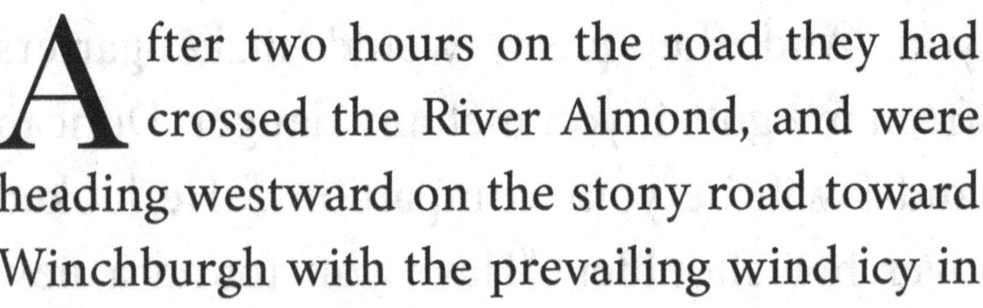

After two hours on the road they had crossed the River Almond, and were heading westward on the stony road toward Winchburgh with the prevailing wind icy in their faces. John was seriously regretting his foolhardy bravado in agreeing to this trip.

I should have stayed in bed, he thought, wrapping the folds of his cloak closer around his body. With every stride that Dirk took his chest tightened, and his muscles ached with the effort of holding himself into the saddle after so many days of inactivity.

Above his head, the sky was that ominous heavy grey that often preceded snow. But surely it would not snow this early in December?

Yet it was only moments later that he felt the first soft flake against his cheek, then spied another expiring quietly on his wool-covered arm. His mouth set in a line. *'Tis my fault for thinking about it.*

He pushed Dirk forward, alongside Margaret's mount and spoke in low tones. "Do ye know if there is somewhere before Linlithgow that we could shelter, should this snow impede our progress?"

Margaret cast a glance at him, eyes flashing silver. "'Twill be fine." She lifted her chin. "'Tis not that far to the palace. Our horses are strong. There's no need to worry."

But even as she spoke, the wind gusted and swirled around them, throwing icy crystals into their faces and causing John's eyes to close against the blast. By the time he opened them again, blinking the snowflakes from his lashes, the road ahead had a sheen of white, and the bushes and trees to the side of the road were taking on a ghostly hue, as if some heavenly wastrel had thrown precious salt everywhere, like scattered seed on freshly tilled ground.

The change in the weather appeared to cause Margaret to reconsider. "But if it gets worse, Lord Seton's keep at Niddry isn't far," she added.

Within ten minutes, their horses were struggling through ankle-deep snow, and forward progress slowed as every step became an effort.

However, Duncan's mount, an over-sized pony with a thick coat that somehow repelled the snow, was much more sure-footed in the slippery going. On a wider part of the road, the manservant trotted back to them and addressed his master. "Sire, do ye want me to ride ahead and find somewhere we can shelter?"

John caught Margaret's eye. Her face flushed by the frosty wind and her chin tucked into the collar of her cloak, she did not speak, just gave the merest hint of a nod.

"Aye, Duncan, if ye would. Lady Carwood tells me Niddry Castle is close by. See if you can rouse the constable and get him to make ready for us."

CHAPTER 8

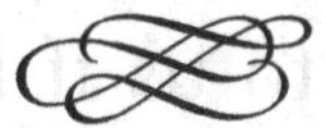

It seemed to take forever for them to reach Lord Seton's castle, slogging through snow as thick as porridge which grasped at the horse's feet like mermaids clutching at drowning sailors. But, eventually, Margaret spotted a wan light flickering off to their left, and as they drew closer, the shadowy wall of the castle hove into view.

A round tower was set into the corner of the curtain wall, with a stout timber gate below it. All was eerily silent in the falling snow, and, despite the lit window, high in the keep, Margaret began to wonder if the place had been abandoned. "Would Duncan have ridden back to us if he'd failed to gain admittance?"

"Aye." John's voice was faint, and the intake of cold air set him off into a fit of coughing again.

"The sooner we get you into the warm, the better," Margaret said, scanning the walls again, looking for signs of life. *Surely there should be a watchman?* 'Twould not be like Lord Seton to leave the castle undefended. And Duncan should have alerted the constable to look out for them.

As if sparked magically by her thoughts, the gate by the watchtower suddenly opened, and a large man clad in a dark woollen coat and carrying a long wooden pole emerged, then halted abruptly at the sight of them.

"Good day, sire," John greeted him. Somehow, he managed to put some strength into his voice, despite his coughing fit moments earlier. "I am John Stewart, Laird of Fincastle, and this is Lady Carwood, who is handmaid to the queen. My manservant should ha' alerted you that we are in need o' shelter?"

Blinking, the man stared at them blankly for a moment. "Nay, we have had no visitors since Monday."

Margaret glanced worriedly at John, who was coughing again. "We are en-route to Stirling for the Prince's baptism, but have been caught out by this snowstorm. Can we impose upon your hospitality until the weather abates?"

The man frowned, and glanced back at the castle. Pressing his lips together, he peered at the falling snow behind them before replying. "Aye, I guess. But," he raised a shoulder, "Lord Seton took most of the staff with him to Stirling, and I am off," he pointed his staff into the snowstorm, "to the village yonder. My old mother has a hole in her roof and the snow comes in. Ye'll have ta get Jenny to look after ye."

Spinning on his heel, he threw open the gate and ushered them through. "Lock it behind ye, if ye will. The horses can go in the barn wi' Tam, and there's a fire in the great hall to keep ye warm. Now," he wrapped his cloak around his shoulders, "I must away!"

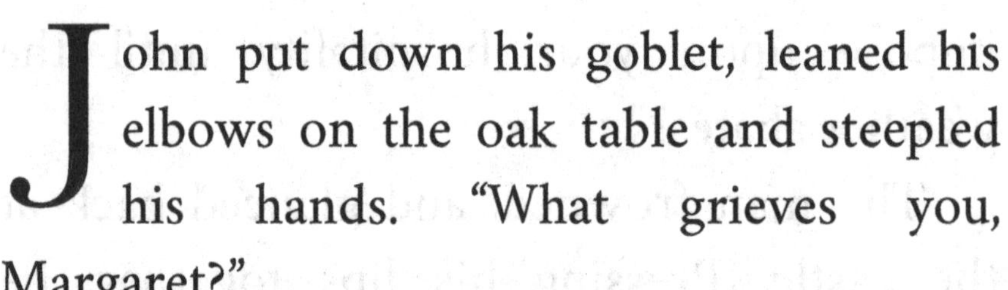

John put down his goblet, leaned his elbows on the oak table and steepled his hands. "What grieves you, Margaret?"

Her jaw tightened, and she raised her eyes to meet his. The skin on her face glowed in the soft light cast from thick, creamy candles, which scented the air of Niddry great hall with beeswax and made it feel like a sanctuary from the snowstorm raging outside.

"Duncan," she finally answered.

Above their heads, stout roof timbers supported the lofty ceiling, and underfoot, rush-covered flagstones softened the tread of the maid, who reappeared at that moment to gather the remains of the cold meat, bread and cheese she'd set out for them earlier. The girl nodded at the fire. "Ye'd be warmer at the hearth, m'lord and lady. I'll bring you a spiced wine posset if you take yerselves over there."

Being inside, and out of the wind, had somewhat eased the tightness in John's chest, but he found himself looking forward to the hot drink. "Shall we?" he asked, gesturing at the carved wooden chairs that flanked the large fireplace. Logs glowed in the grate, crackling occasionally as orange flames licked at the soot in the chimney.

Margaret nodded, and they were soon seated either side of the hearth. Holding his hands towards the heat, John gave his companion a questioning look. "Duncan?"

"Why is he not here? What can have happened to him?" She balled her fingers into fists. "He should have reached Niddry well before us. Could he…" she faltered, chewing on her lip.

"Could he…?" John prompted.

She swallowed, then met his gaze. "Could he have been set upon by reivers?"

"Here?" If she hadn't looked so serious—and worried—John would have laughed. Instead, he shook his head and kept his expression carefully neutral. He could not let her see that he himself had concerns about his manservant. "We are too far north. More like he found himself a refuge from the storm and is holed up until daybreak."

"You think?"

"Aye. That man knows how to fight his way out of a scrape, should he need to. And his pony is as surefooted as a goat. He'll be safe and dry somewhere, don't ye worry," he added, aware he was reassuring himself as much as her.

The heavy-timbered door of the hall opened and the maid reappeared, causing a draught to swirl around their feet, and setting John off into another coughing fit.

Jenny bobbed a curtsey, and handed them their drinks. "Will there be anything else?" she asked. "I've lit the fires to warm your chambers. We break our fast after first light in the morn, there will be oats and milk set out in the hall here. And young Tam has seen to your beasties so there's no need for ye to go back outside into the cold."

"Perhaps some hot water with honey and lemon for the laird?" Margaret suggested.

"This posset will be fine," John wheezed,

then cleared his throat and took a sip. The spicy aroma made his nostrils flare, and the concoction warmed and soothed as it made its way to his stomach, relieving the tickle that had caused his cough. He nodded. "'Tis good, thank ye."

When the maid had gone, Margaret cradled her drink in both hands, gazing into the fire, her brow furrowed and her lips pursed.

"My lady?" John made his enquiry into a question.

"It's just… I've known reivers to attack, even in weather like this."

"We are safe here in the castle." John waved an arm at the thick stone walls that surrounded them.

"But Duncan is not."

"He is but one man on a hairy garron. A thief would go after richer pickings, believe me. If they could even find him in this storm!" he added, trying to make light of her worries.

But her countenance did not ease.

"My lady," he pulled his chair closer, then leaned forward. "What worries ye? I can see there is more to this than concern for my manservant."

She glanced at him, then stared down at her drink again, as if debating with herself. After a long pause, she let loose a deep sigh. "We lost my parents in a storm like this. Years ago." A gust of wind whistled around the battlements and rattled the leaded windows of the hall, as if illustrating her story.

"I remember you said they'd died. But you didn't say how."

Taking a pull from her goblet, she inclined her head, "They were returning home from Edinburgh when reivers set upon them and chased them to the river. They tried to cross, but it was in spate, and they were swept away." Her voice had lowered to a whisper. "'Twas days later afore they found the bodies."

"I'm so sorry." He put a hand over hers. "Truly."

~

Margaret met his gaze, her eyes misty. "Thank you, sire."

"How old were ye when it happened?" he asked, concern furrowing his brow.

"Twelve, Janet was thirteen."

He frowned, and sat back. "You'd not reached your majority?"

She shook her head. "Our father's friend —we called him uncle, but he was no blood relation—took wardship of us. But he…" she tailed off, pushing back the memories, and taking a deep breath before she continued. "He was not a nice man. In the end, the courts intervened, and declared that he had to marry one of us."

"Your sister, I assume?"

"Yes. Every day I give thanks that it was

not me. Yet I also feel guilty that I was able to escape that house into the service of our Queen. So I remember my sister every day in my prayers." She took another swallow of the posset, as if trying to also swallow the guilt that had arisen anew with talking about it. "But Janet had his child recently, and seems to have found some happiness in that."

"Does that mean the story has a happy ending?"

Happy? She ruminated on that for a moment. *Was* she happy? The royal court did not seem so safe now as it had when she first arrived. "Of sorts. T'would have been better had that man never entered our lives."

"But if that had happened, you would not be here," with an arm he indicated the large room with its wood-panelled walls and faded tapestries, "sampling the delights of Niddry in the snow, and looking forward to performing at the Prince's baptism."

She chuckled. He certainly had a knack

for lightening her mood, and made it hard for her to remember he was a miscreant. "You speak truth, sire. I am glad to have served my Queen, and I know I have given some help and comfort to her. I would not have missed that."

Fincastle had relaxed in his chair, arms resting on the sides and feet pointing towards the fire. Perhaps with this easing of the mood between them, now would be a good time to ask him about the plot?

She sat taller in her chair and clasped her hands together. "So now you know my secrets, sire. Is it time for you to tell me yours?"

He gave her a sharp look, suddenly alert.

Margaret held her tongue, watching the emotions war on his face. One thing she had learned at court was that silence was often the best way to provoke speech in others.

Finally the laird seemed to reach a decision. He jumped to his feet, and began to pace from one side of the hearth to the other. "I need your help, Lady Carwood."

"My help?" That was *not* what she'd expected to hear.

"Aye. I find myself in a dangerous situation, and I need someone with the ear of the queen, who can pass on a warning if need be."

Her brain spinning, Margaret stared at him. "A warning?" she repeated.

"Aye. I—" He stopped for a moment and rubbed a hand behind his neck. "By accident, I overheard some of the lords plotting against the king—"

"The king?" Margaret interrupted. "But I thought..." Her hand flew to her mouth. *Have a care! You nearly admitted to overhearing them.*

He gave her a keen look. "Aye, the king. They see him as a threat to the queen, and plan his demise."

So it was not the queen they were plotting against. A huge weight lifted from Margaret's shoulders, and she almost sighed with relief.

"I had to pretend to join their scheme." He grimaced. "It was that, or Bothwell's sword through my guts."

Lost for words, Margaret stared at him. Bothwell was certainly audacious enough to spear someone he considered an enemy. It seemed Fincastle was not the knave she thought. *Unless...*

Unless he was bluffing her, or playing her for a fool?

The laird sat down again, almost as suddenly as he'd stood up, then took her hand and looked into her eyes. "Will you be my ally? Pass word to the queen once I find out the details of their plot?" He clenched his jaw. "'Tis not right, what they plan for the king."

It was this last statement that convinced

her of his integrity. "Even if the king plots against the queen?"

"Does not make regicide right." His face took on a bullish look.

Like the pieces in a backgammon game, something clicked into place inside her, and she placed her other hand on top of his. "I will help you. If I can. Remember, I am a mere chamberwoman."

"But you have the ear of the queen. That is of most import."

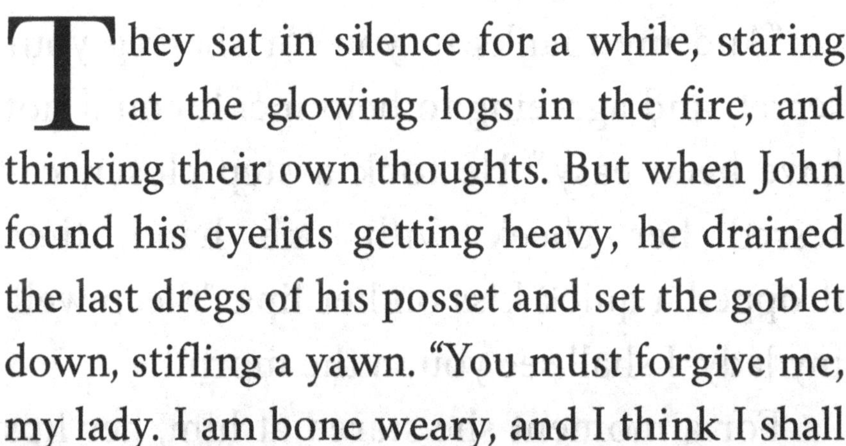

They sat in silence for a while, staring at the glowing logs in the fire, and thinking their own thoughts. But when John found his eyelids getting heavy, he drained the last dregs of his posset and set the goblet down, stifling a yawn. "You must forgive me, my lady. I am bone weary, and I think I shall fall asleep here, should I sit much longer." He levered himself to his feet.

Margaret jumped up. "I shall away to my chamber also. We can set off to look for Duncan at dawn."

"Unless he finds us first," John replied, ever the optimist.

With a rustle of her skirts, she made her way across the hall, and John followed, catching a hint of vanilla in her wake.

Outside her chamber, she turned to face him, her face shadowed in the flickering light of a wall sconce. "My thanks to you, sire, for allaying my fears."

"And my thanks to you for sharing your secret, and agreeing to help me. It could not have been easy." He took a step closer, caressed her cheek with one hand, then dropped a quick kiss on her lips. "Sleep well, my lady. I shall see you in the morn."

For a moment she stared at him, her lips parted in surprise. Then her manners seemed to re-assert themselves. "And you, my lord. Good night."

John strode off to his bedchamber, a smile tickling his cheeks. With his secret shared and a pact made, he would sleep well tonight.

CHAPTER 9

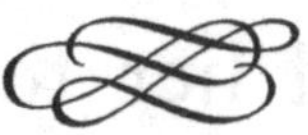

SATURDAY 14TH DECEMBER 1566

But John did not sleep as well as he expected.

As he tossed and turned, he blamed an over-soft mattress and an over-cold room, despite the memories that would not leave his brain in peace: Flames licking across a distant roof. Margaret's face, glowing in the candle-light. Lizzy's face, also aglow, standing in the warm light from a window as she told him of the child she bore. The dread in his throat as he ran in slow motion towards a burning building. Margaret sinking into the murky depths of the loch. The strong hands that grasped his doublet to stop him throwing himself futilely into the inferno. The dead weight of Margaret as he desperately pulled her to the surface. The coarseness of the earth he tossed onto the wooden casket nestling at the bottom of a grave…

When morning finally came, he was glad, despite the cloud that mired his head and the grit that filled his eyes. For it allowed him to escape those nightmarish dreams and face the future, rather than the past. But as he dunked his face in the bowl of frigid water on the washstand in his chamber, he paused, water dripping off his chin. What *was* it that had provoked those memories?

As he dried his face on a scrap of cloth, he recalled the images of Margaret that had been interspersed with the flashbacks of the fire. Could it be because of the emotions she'd stirred up? *That must be it,* he decided.

If he wanted her help against the plotters, perhaps disturbed sleep was the penalty.

With a grimace, he grabbed his saddle bag and went in search of breakfast.

With fingers that felt like blocks of ice inside her leather gloves, Margaret checked her horse's girth, before Tam led him to the mounting block. The morning air smelled of woodsmoke and dirty stables, with little trace of last night's snowstorm apart from some clumps of snow still clinging to the ground on the leeward side of the castle.

The temperature must have risen overnight. So why was she so cold? And then she remembered that she had not eaten any breakfast because of her worry about Duncan, who had still not arrived. *That must be it.*

At the other side of the stable yard, John

was grim-faced and ashen, as he strapped his bag behind Dirk's saddle. *He has not slept either,* Margaret realised. He must worry about his manservant as she did, despite his words to the contrary.

She was pushing her calfskin boots into the stirrups when her horse threw his head up, its nostrils flaring. She grasped at the reins in panic, visions of Ember and her headlong gallop at Holyrood making her clamp her legs onto the beast and causing him to shuffle sideways and nearly knock the groom over.

But then there was a shout from outside the walls, and banging at the watchtower door. *Reivers!* Margaret thought, her hand flying to her mouth and her throat seizing as the horse underneath her fidgeted warily, obviously sensing her distress.

Tam hurried over to the gate, closely followed by the laird, whose hand was on his sword hilt. But Margaret relaxed and began to breathe again when, after some brief en-quiries, they admitted a shamefaced Duncan, cap in hand and shoulders sagging.

He is safe! Relief washed over Margaret like a wave, and she felt lighter than she had in days.

"I'm sorry, sire." Duncan kept his eyes fixed studiously on his hands. "I saw lights through the snowstorm and ended up at the wrong castle. Newliston, it was called, south of here, home to a family called Dundas. They told me that everyone from Niddry had gone to Stirling for the baptism, and said that you and the lady would surely arrive at Newliston instead. Except you did not, but by then it was dark and…"

John stepped in front of him and raised a hand, stopping him mid-sentence. "'Tis fine, Duncan, you are here now, and we are both well. Think nothing of it." He turned to Dirk and sprung aboard in one easy movement.

"Let us away now, for 'tis a long ride to Stirling, and the light fades early."

❧

But progress was slow on the boggy tracks, and it took them two hours to reach the royal palace at Linlithgow. By then, John had begun to cough again, and, while they watered the horses and waited for a servant to bring them some victuals for the rest of their journey, Margaret approached him.

"Sire, 'tis still some twenty miles to Stirling. And you are not yet fully recovered. Should we rest here today, and continue our journey tomorrow?"

He regarded her from under his hat. This was a changed woman from the one who'd been so desperate to get to Stirling and her queen that she'd tried to leave Edinburgh on her own. Could she…? But no. 'Twas too much to hope.

"'Tis the Sabbath tomorrow, and we will be frowned upon if we travel." He glanced up at the sky. "And we do not know what tomorrow's weather will bring. After that 'tis only one more day till the baptism. I would that we ride on while we can. But is there some place we might aim for as a way point, and perhaps stay the night if 'tis too far after all?"

Looking up, as if plotting their route on the clouds, she pondered for a moment. "The queen often stops at Callendar, near Falkirk. That would be about half-way."

"Then let us ride for Callendar. And Stirling beyond, if God wills."

Night had fallen and the stars were out by the time their little party reached the solid ramparts of Stirling Castle. *We made it.* John was weary to his bones, and could think of nothing save a hot drink and a soft bed.

But still he gazed in awe at the walls of the royal residence, which must be two yards thick and disappeared into the darkness around the side of the hill which topped the little town.

If he'd thought that Craigmillar was a good, solid castle and Edinburgh impressive and impenetrable, then Stirling was dramatic and imposing in the extreme, and looked to be the largest by some long way. *'Twill impress the English dignitaries who come for the baptism.*

Thanks to the stories Lady Carwood had told—which had made their journey pass more quickly—John now had a much better understanding of some of the politics and intrigue of the royal court. He had also seen a different side to Margaret. Less the prickly rose, she had been more like a sweet peony or fragrant gillyflower. It was as if the sharing of secrets last night had opened her up like petals in sunshine. He liked her like that.

Margaret had halted her horse and was frowning at some structure built on rough ground beside the approach to the castle. "I think that must be for our masque," she pointed at the wooden framework.

"Aye, ye may be right." John's hands tightened on the reins. "And a bonfire beyond, if I'm not mistaken." It was close. *Too close.* He would ask for it to be moved.

"We can explore on the morrow. And rehearse," she said, "but for now, let us eat and rest. 'Twill be a long week, methinks."

CHAPTER 10

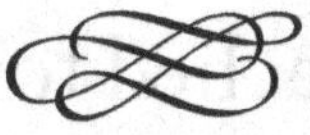

MONDAY 16TH DECEMBER 1566

The page gave a bow and swung the door open, announcing, "The Queen of Scots, my lord."

Mary swept into her husband's bedchamber, and stopped short, her eyes widening. There was a sickly smell in the room, something she couldn't identify. But whatever it was, it made her nostrils itch.

Typically, Darnley was still abed, even though it was past noon, and the window drapes had only partially been opened. She strode across and pulled at the heavy fabric.

"Why have your servants not opened the curtains? I shall get the housekeeper to have words with them."

"Leave them, wife!" Henry's voice cracked, and he reached for a silver goblet by his bedside. "I want no visitors."

The chastisement for the tone of his address to his queen was on her lips when Mary noticed the red weal at the side of his mouth. She gasped. "Has someone been fighting with you? I shall have them thrown in the dungeon."

He flicked his hand at her as if swatting an unwelcome fly. "I have not been fighting. But I am tired and unwell. Why do you visit?" Then a lustful gleam appeared in his eyes. "Or do you wish for us to make another baby, in case anything happens to young James?"

Having been brought up in the French court, Mary was well schooled in hiding her feelings. But it took an effort to hide the revulsion she felt at this suggestion. "Nothing will happen to the prince," she said firmly, smoothing the rich brocade of her damask gown. "I came to ask if you will meet with the foreign dignitaries this evening? There is to be a reception before dinner."

Lying back against his pillows, Darnley placed the back of his hand against his forehead. "I do not feel strong enough to appear in public."

If she thought she wouldn't have been seen by him, Mary would have rolled her eyes at his histrionics. She was sure that if he thought there was something in it for him, he would make a miraculous recovery.

Clenching her fists, she played the ace that she had been holding in reserve ever since the masque at Craigmillar. "Even if that appearance is where you are introduced as the future King of Scots?"

"The crown matrimonial?" A moment of

lust flashed in his eyes before he hooded them again.

"Oui." She managed not to hesitate before replying.

"You will make me king?" He looked sceptical. "Now? Why now?"

"Not right now, but after the baptism. Once James is proclaimed Prince of Scotland. As his father, you are king." That part was not a lie. Due to her status, he was called king. But he would not inherit the throne without being given the crown matrimonial, which was something he had chafed for, ever since their marriage. *Something that will never happen.*

Mary had learned lessons from her cousin, Elizabeth of England, who kept the men of her court dangling with flirtation and promises. But the English queen showed no sign of giving up her throne to a man—which is what would surely happen if she married. And Mary knew the same would happen to *her* if she made her husband co-regent. He would conspire to have her removed, one way or another, and he would proclaim himself king.

"I shall send the doctor to attend to you," she said mildly, trailing a finger down one of the ornately carved bedposts and then turning for the door. "So you are recovered in time for the reception."

Margaret would be proud of my acting skills, she thought as she departed his malodorous chamber. But if it took the promise of the crown to make Darnley attend the baptism, she would do whatever was required to gain his compliance. For that would seal James' legitimacy in the eyes of the populace, and dispel any rumours to the contrary. Whatever it took. *My son is worth it.*

~

"Now!" cried John, and a wave of unrecognisable soldiers with black faces and flowing dark robes came screaming towards him, brandishing three-pronged spears.

They had almost reached the wooden walls of the makeshift tower John was standing on when Margaret, standing beside him and looking effortlessly regal, raised both arms. "Begone!" At the same time, John stooped and pretended to fire the cannon—brought specially from Edinburgh Castle—which sat beside them.

As if impaled on invisible pikes, the demons fell to the ground, and mostly lay still, apart from a few that groaned and writhed in fake death throes.

"Bravo!" Sebastian Pages walked towards them, clapping his hands as the fallen soldiers began to rouse. He raised a finger at John. "But next time without the stage directions?"

"Mayhap Duncan could hide on the knoll beside them, and tell them when to attack?"

"Oui, that could work." Bastian stroked at his beard, then glanced up at the sun. "D'accord. We shall have one more rehearsal. After we have eaten something. The men will be hungry."

Sitting on a convenient rock in the scrubby hillside before the castle, John took a bite from the meat pie a kitchen maid had delivered, and glanced sideways at Margaret. "You make a good queen."

She laughed. "And you are every inch the descendant of Robert the Bruce."

It was his turn to smile. "I have me some regrets that I ever told you that."

Unbidden, a memory of their kiss at Craigmillar found its way into his brain, and he coughed into his hand to cover his discomfiture.

Margaret's cheeks were flushed, and, for

a second, he wondered if her mind had strayed in the same direction. But then he dismissed the thought as too fanciful.

With a gloved hand, she indicated the troops arrayed in front of them. "Do you think they are ready? And will they perform as well when they have an audience of nobles and royalty?"

"They have an audience already," John said, pointing at the road leading to the town below the castle rock, where a number of interested townsfolk had been watching the morning's goings-on. He frowned. "But where *are* the lords? I have seen no-one today."

"Hunting," Margaret replied succinctly. "You were still abed when they left this morning."

"Ah." John hung his head. After yet another disturbed night, Duncan had let him sleep on, and it had been some hours past dawn when he had finally risen.

"Did you wish to go with them? I am sure you could join them even now. They have gone to Saint Ninians, I believe."

She had misinterpreted his upset, but he would not set her right. "'Tis naught. Hunting is not my favourite pastime." He raised an eyebrow at her, making her laugh. "I prefer acting."

Doctor Nau held his cap in his hand, his eyes downcast. Wan winter light from the nearby window illuminated his face with its olive skin, strong brow and wide mouth. "I am afraid to report, ma'am, that I believe the king has the great pox."

Mary gasped. "How can that be?"

The doctor lifted a shoulder in that eloquent way that the French had, a gesture that spoke volumes while the lips said nothing.

Then the voices of courtiers gossiping in

corridors swam, unbidden, into Mary's mind, and she remembered the rumours of Darnley's carousing and whoring—with both men and women. Her spirits sank. "Will—will 'e be well enough to attend the baptism? And the reception this evening?"

"I have recommended treatment with a unguent of sarsaparilla, and daily sweat baths to rid the body of the noxious elements. It pains me to say it, but I have found no real cure for the pox." He looked up, a glimmer of hope in his dark eyes. "*Yet.* I have high hopes for the salve, 'tis the first time I have used it on a patient in the early stages of the disease. Pray to God for a good outcome."

~

Bothwell pulled his horse to a halt, its sides heaving, then quickly swung the bow from his shoulder and let loose an arrow. To his annoyance, it flew past the beast and embedded itself in a tree. Growling with anger, he was about to chase after the stag again when he was interrupted by the arrival of another rider.

"Good day, Lord Bothwell." William Maitland drew up beside him in the small clearing. "I hoped we might have a short discussion."

"If you make it quick." Bothwell gestured at the thicket ahead of them. "I have a stag to catch. What do you wish to talk about?"

"About our—ahem—royal problem." Grey eyebrows raised sardonically.

Ah. That piqued the earl's interest. "The subject of our Craigmillar agreement?" He checked the woods around them to ensure there were no flapping ears to overhear.

"The very same. Our Craigmillar bond bound us to rid the queen of the embarrassment her husband causes. And now the scuttlebutt around the castle has it that he is sick with the great pox. Might there be anything we can do whilst we are here?"

"The pox?" Bothwell shook his head, his lips pressed together. "We should warn the queen, so she does not lie with him."

"There is no danger of that." Maitland spoke firmly, as if sure of his ground.

So she does not entertain the king. Bothwell had guessed as much, but to hear it from her secretary was interesting. He rubbed his hands together and a smile twitched at his mouth. "Perhaps if he comes hunting with us next time, an arrow could… go astray. Some of the junior lords are bad marksmen. Or my injury could be acting up, causing my aim to spoil…"

"But not until after the baptism tomorrow. We need to get the prince christened, with the king present, and dispel any doubt as to his parentage."

Bothwell had forgotten that part—the rumours that Mary's secretary, Riccio, had fathered her bairn. As if that popinjay would have been interested in a woman! But her friendship with her former secretary had caused gossip, and that gossip—and jealousy—had been enough to get Riccio killed by a cabal of her lords. A conspiracy which had also included her husband… "Is that why she does not lie with the king? Because of Riccio?" The earl almost licked his lips at the thought.

Raising a palm, Maitland observed his companion levelly. "You might conclude such a thing. I could not possibly guess at the queen's motivations."

Said like a true politician. Bothwell narrowed his eyes. "I will look for an opportunity, then. But after the ceremony."

Maitland nodded, then turned his horse to face the nearest path. "Now, where went that stag you were after?"

Margaret touched the queen's arm, briefly. "Ma'am, we should go to dinner. The ambassadors will be waiting."

"Just one moment." Mary leaned into the little prince's ornately carved crib, and laid the back of her hand on his forehead. Then she frowned. "Do you think 'e has a fever?" Her eyes widened. "Could 'e have caught the pox from his father?"

"Ma'am, the king has been nowhere near the nursery ever since he arrived. I have it on good authority from the nursemaid." He may have been the child's father, but Darnley seemed entirely uninterested in the bairn.

"But 'e could still have a fever, yes?" It was obvious from the way Mary's French accent had thickened that she was concerned about her son.

"Let me see." Margaret felt the baby's brow, which was pleasantly warm, but not hot. "He seems fine to me." She beckoned the nanny over. "What think you, Jessie?"

The plump woman picked the boy up and cradled him in her arms, then tested his skin. "Ma'am, if I thought there were anything wrong with His Grace I'd 'a been the first to tell you. Or get thon doctor. But the bairn is in fine fettle, I'd swear my life on it."

Smoothing aside a curl of hair that lay on his temple, Mary kissed the tips of her fingers, then placed them on James' lips. "Very well. Sleep well, my little son. We shall see you in the morning for your baptism, your mother and your father both."

Margaret caught Jessie's eye, and she could see from the servant's expression that she was of the same opinion—that the king had no intention at all of attending the baptism, preferring instead to leave the little prince's parentage in doubt, thus strengthening his case to be regent, should anything happen to Mary.

But the queen seemed determined to think the best of the man, and Margaret could say nothing. *Events will tell,* she thought. On the morrow, the queen would discover once more that she could not rely on the king, that he was self-serving and not to be trusted. Perhaps this time she would have had enough.

Even so, she can do naught, a little voice niggled. Mary could not divorce him without making James illegitimate in Catholic eyes, which was why the lords were plotting against Darnley.

"Come," the queen beckoned for Margaret to follow her, "we must attend the reception."

"Yes, ma'am." Margaret dropped a curtsey. As she accompanied her mistress out of the nursery and down the flagstone-paved corridor that led to the hall where the evening's event would take place, she wrestled with her conscience. *Should I tell the queen?* Would she want to know?

If the lords were successful in their plot, perhaps it was better that the queen did *not* know, so she could deny any responsibility.

But what if the queen somehow got caught up in it, like she had been in the plot to kill Riccio? What if she was hurt or killed? Mayhap it would be better if she was forewarned.

Then an image of John's guileless face and clear blue eyes swam into Margaret's mind. If she told the queen about the plot, would that get the laird into trouble? Or would Bothwell spear him for his disloyalty?

Margaret flinched, imagining a sword impaling her innards. *No,* she decided. Not yet. *Not till I know 'tis safe for the laird.*

CHAPTER 11

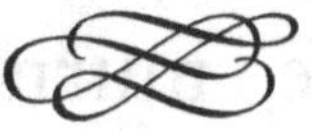

TUESDAY 17TH DECEMBER 1566

Mary ground her teeth. From her seat in the north transept, she surveyed the stone chapel with its gilded altar, stained glass windows, and a large gold font in pride of place. The ostentatious piece was a christening gift from her cousin Elizabeth, the Queen of England, delivered by her ambassador, the Earl of Bedford. Elizabeth, of course, had declined to attend the momentous event.

As, it seemed, had Mary's husband. Beckoning a page, she hissed at him, "Go and see if the king needs help to dress. He should 'ave been here five minutes ago."

Carrying his staff of office, Archbishop Hamilton sidled over to her. "Will the king be attending?" he murmured, his breath smelling of vinegar and cloves.

"I 'ope so. I have sent a page to fetch him."

"Very well. We shall wait."

Her stomach in knots, Mary passed the time by scrutinising the occupants of the carved wooden pews in the nave, thankful for once that their Protestant snobbery had stopped most of her lords—and the English ambassador—from attending this Catholic ritual. 'Twas better they did not see her embarrassment.

Even her faithful Earl of Bothwell had chosen to miss this part of the baptismal celebrations, despite the fact that he had been instrumental in organising much of the festivities.

When the page came back—alone—a few

minutes later, Mary had to fight back tears. *Could he not even do this for me? With the promise of the crown he wants so much?*

"The king is ill abed," the page whispered, cap in hand and eyes fixed on the floor. "He says he is too sick to attend."

Mary took a moment to compose herself, clasping her hands together in her lap and breathing deeply. Then she lengthened her back, lifted her chin, and gave the clergy the signal to begin. *I am the queen,* she told herself. *I do not need that man to legitimise my son.* But the hammering of her heart gave lie to her thoughts.

In the transept of the glittering chapel, a bishop swung his thurible, releasing the aroma of incense. It tickled Mary's nostrils and filtered up to the rafters, taking with it her fervent prayers…

Her face flushed, Margaret laughed up at him. "For a sheep farmer, you dance a good gavotte. I thought you told Bastian you were no dancer?"

John lifted a shoulder. "It takes a good partner to make a good dancer."

She dropped her head at that.

I have embarrassed her. He found it interesting that such a sophisticated member of the royal court would be so easily flustered. But it made her seem more human, somehow, and perhaps more agreeable than the waspish lady he'd first encountered. "What say you to a walk around the castle walls? To cool off." To illustrate his point, he passed a handkerchief over his sweat-beaded brow.

In answer, she spun on her heel and headed for the door. When he caught up with her, she was taking a velvet cloak from a servant, and held out another for him. "'Twill be cold on the battlements."

He slung the garment over his arm. "I am too warm right now." But almost as soon as they stepped outside, the cold bit into his lungs, seizing his chest and nipping at his nostrils. With a shiver, he wrapped the mantle around his shoulders, and followed Margaret up the stone steps that led to the wall walk.

"Evening, sire, madam," a sentry greeted them as they walked past the first turret, his breath clouding above his head.

John slipped Margaret's hand into the crook of his elbow and led her further along, away from listening ears. "How is the queen? She seemed in fine form at the dance."

Margaret darted a quick glance at him. "She is putting a good face on it. But the king not attending Prince James' baptism has pained her greatly."

"I hear he has the pox. I assume he is too ill to join in the festivities."

"You are too kind to the man. I am sure

he could have made it to the christening at least, if he had been a good husband to the queen. He is not so indisposed that he cannot stand. Some say he is just too vain to be seen in public with sores on his face."

They came to a crenellation with a good view over the moonlit countryside beyond the castle, and John stopped, the king forgotten. All was still, the fields and forests a monochrome painting in shades of dark blue. He pointed outwards. "Tis a magnificent panorama." Somewhere in the distance, a cow lowed, its call plaintive in the cold air.

Margaret stepped in beside him. "True, but I am sure the castle builders did not envisage this use for the allure."

"The allure?" Looking into her shadowed eyes, he thought for a moment she meant *her* allure.

"That is what they call the wall walk." She scuffed a foot on the stone paving beneath them. "The allure. The arrow slits let archers aim at attackers, and the crenels allow soldiers to pour burning oil," she indicated an empty brazier to his right, "on their enemies."

He flinched involuntarily at the thought of the fire, and her brow furrowed as she glanced between him and the metal grate. "You asked for the bonfire to be moved yesterday. Is there something… about fire…?" She tailed off, as if realising how direct she was being, and shook her head. "Forgive me. I should not have asked."

As Margaret stared at the craggy planes of his face, it clouded, like mist cloaking a mountain, and he pulled himself to a more upright position, staring into the distance with his shoulders tense and his hands braced on the parapet. "Aye. You are right. There is something."

Margaret stifled her natural impulse to fill the silence. She could almost *see* the thoughts warring on his countenance, and words from her would not hurry that process. Indeed, they might halt it.

"My house. *Our* house, at Fincastle, as was. I came down the glen from the quarry late one afternoon to find the place in flames, my wife trapped inside." The muscles in his jaw clamped, and he put his head in his hands. "A cart with gunpowder destined for the limeworks had exploded and set light to the roof." His next words were muffled. "I could do nothing."

Margaret put a hand on his arm. "I'm so sorry."

It took a minute for him to regain his composure. "Forgive me," he said, wiping his palm across his face.

Unaccustomed to seeing men show their emotions, her heart twisted. "There is nothing to forgive. 'Tis natural to grieve."

His eyes were bright. "Thank ye." Then he straightened, taking a deep breath. "So now ye know all my secrets, my lady."

She held his gaze. "And you mine."

"Aye." He took her hands in his, then dropped a quick kiss on her knuckles. "I will keep them safe." Tucking her arm in his, he started walking back towards the hall. "Now, shall we see if there is a pavane for me to mangle? I shall try not to stand on your toes."

They had only gone a few strides when Margaret suddenly stopped.

"What is it?" he asked.

"I just realised something." She blinked up at him, almost in awe, trying to understand the fullness she felt in her chest.

His eyebrows drew together, asking the question.

Then, instead of answering, she surprised herself by reaching her hands up behind his neck and drawing him into a kiss, one that was long and deep and sweet like honey.

When they finally broke apart, John's face was beatific. He ran a finger down the side of her cheek, causing every nerve in her body to tingle. "What did you realise?" he whispered.

"It's—I—I think," she could hardly form the words, "for the first time ever in my life, I feel truly safe in the company of a man."

His frown deepened. "You have not felt safe with men before this?"

"No, not completely." She shook her head. "Not that I can recall."

He drew her into his arms. "Does this feel better? Or worse?" A hint of uncertainty flashed across his shadowed face.

Allowing herself just to *feel*, to acknowledge her emotions, she stood quietly for a moment, assessing her mood. *Why* did she feel safer? Was it because he had shared his secrets with her? Or his emotion? It was like there was a thread connecting them now, one that had not been there before. "Better," she decided, gazing into his eyes.

Somewhere along the wall walk, a sentry coughed, and that broke the spell between them. "Pavane?" John asked, taking her arm again. "Shall we show those English lords how *not* to do it?"

She laughed, her mood buoyant. "Lead on, Laird Fincastle."

CHAPTER 12

WEDNESDAY 18TH DECEMBER 1566

The next morning, John awoke refreshed for the first time in days, his soul lighter than it had felt in years. As he splashed his face with water from a china bowl on the washstand, he churned things over, trying to work out what was different, and why there had been no nightmares to endure.

Then he realised. The bad dreams had started the night they spent in Niddry Castle. Margaret had opened up about her fears, and told him about her parents and her guardian. But he had held back one of his secrets until last night, when he had finally told her about the fire and his wife. It was as if he had not been able to rest properly until he shared everything with her.

His hands stilled, and he leaned on the dresser and stared out of the small window in the tiny room he'd been allocated. It had felt good to talk with her, to have someone who understood how things were. *Someone who is on my side.* They made a good team.

Fastening the last buttons on his doublet, John skipped down the stone-flagged stairs and stepped out into the courtyard. But then the murmur of agitated voices from somewhere nearby halted his foot in mid stride, and some instinct made him shrink back into a nearby doorway.

"We cannot trust him," a man was saying. "He has been seen with the queen's chamberwoman, the red-haired one."

John's lungs stopped working. *They are talking of me. And Margaret.*

Then the second speaker cut in. "But we cannot assume, just because he is having a dalliance—"

Dalliance? John's guts churned. Whatever he and Margaret had, he was certain it was not a 'dalliance'. But obviously they had been seen together, and gossip had circulated.

"—that the queen will learn of our, ahem, plans."

Maitland! It was the clearing of his throat that helped John recognise the speaker. *And the other must be Bothwell.* Even as he burned to confront them, reason told him to wait, hear what they had to say. He could act later, if action was necessary.

"Well, I do not trust him," Bothwell said.

John could almost hear Maitland's eyebrow raising sardonically. "It seems to me that you do not trust *anyone*, my lord."

The earl spat on the cobbles. "As would

you, if you had seen some of the things I have seen."

"Nevertheless, I urge caution. The laird could be useful to us, with his contacts in Flanders. He was correct. What he proposed would guarantee the—ah—result we desire. Other methods are not so certain, or may leave evidence which would implicate—" Surely a moustache twirling accompanied these words? "—those who would prefer their names not to be associated with such an act."

"I still do not trust him," Bothwell replied stubbornly.

Maitland sucked air through his teeth. "Then set someone to keep watch on him. Report if he is seen with that woman. Or the queen. We need proof of any misdoing."

The earl almost purred. "Gladly. And if he is," a ring of steel sounded in the morning air.

"Quite so, my lord, quite so. Traitors

must be dealt with. But remember, we need proof," he cautioned. "I will not have innocent blood spilled, the queen would not countenance it."

"If you insist."

"I do. Now, shall we eat? I hear there are finnan haddock and devilled eggs to be had in the great hall."

They clattered off across the courtyard, but John stayed hidden, leaning back against the door, his throat aching so much he was sure it had stopped working. His brain also appeared to have seized up, but his one overriding thought was that he needed to speak to Margaret, and warn her of the predicament they were in. But how could he get a message to her, without gossip getting back to Bothwell?

Then with a stifled cry, he grabbed at the stone jamb as the door behind him flew open and Bastian Pages appeared beside him on the step.

"For why are you skulking in doorways, sire? Breakfast is this way. Viens!" The Frenchman caught John by the arm to stop him toppling over, and began to usher him across the courtyard.

"Wait!" John stopped him. It was too soon to go in to the hall, so quickly after the plotters, lest they think he had overheard. But Bastian's arrival had given him an idea. "I need to ask a favour of you, one that will help our masque on the morrow. I want you to get a message to Lady Carwood, for I have a notion of how we can improve the battle scene, and wish us to do one last rehearsal in the tower. Could you get her to meet me there at eleven of the clock? With the final cohort of soldiers?"

"I can ask her, oui. But why do you not ask her yourself?" Bastian gave him a sly look. "I hear you are on good terms."

John gave the Frenchman a hard stare, hoping his acting skills would not desert him. "She is my fellow player in the masque. Of course we have to talk. But that is all there is. She is prickly as a hedgehog and I still grieve for my dear wife." He lifted a finger to the corner of his eye, as if wiping away a tear. At the same time, he sent up a silent prayer of apology for the deception.

Clapping him on the back, Bastian led him towards the hall. "So you say, my friend, so you say. But I will pass on the message for you. Eleven of the clock."

Mary trotted her white palfrey down the hill from the castle, raising a gloved hand to the cheering citizens who lined the route. Behind her, the ambassadors and the lords of court made a colourful spectacle, as they made their way to the hunting grounds for a second day. But this time their monarch was in attendance, and everyone wore their finest riding habits.

On one side she was attended by her ladies-in-waiting, Mary Seton and Mary Fleming; on the other rode her faithful Bothwell. He addressed her now. "Where is your red-haired lady, ma'am? Does she not ride with us?"

"Not today, my lord. She is in final rehearsals for tomorrow's masque. Bastian is all a-flutter."

"Ah, yes." His face hardened. "She was in the masque at Craigmillar, was she not? With that Highlander."

Casting her eyes at the earl, Mary wondered if he was jealous of Laird Fincastle. Might Bothwell have a fancy for Margaret? She could not see it—and the earl had a wife at home, so should not be looking at other women. But his next words did nothing to dispel the notion that he was envious of the laird.

"And now they have starring roles in the christening festivities. Surely someone else is more deserving of the limelight?"

Mary cocked her head. "Do *you* wish to take part, my lord?"

"No, no," Bothwell blustered, "'tis beneath me. But someone else should get a chance."

"Sadly, Bastian finds it hard to get volunteers for his masques." She waved a hand at the ranks of nobility behind them. "Perhaps because the actors have to give up their time, and activities such as this hunt, in order to entertain us. We should be thankful for their dedication."

That seemed to stifle the earl's complaints. But Mary eyed him warily. She was sure that there was something—a spark of some kind—between Margaret and the laird. And, from what she'd seen of John Stewart of Tulliepowries, he was better suited to her chamberwoman than the brash Bothwell would ever be.

But her Lieutenant of the Borders was a strong character, quick to judge and easily angered. She would have to watch that the earl's jealousy did not get out of hand. Margaret would never forgive her if something happened to Fincastle.

~

With a large, sweeping movement, Margaret arranged her arms as if praying, and dropped her head. "They are going to spy on us?" she whispered.

"Yes." Ostentatiously, John did the same, and for a moment they both stood on the top of the masque tower, appearing to be asking for the Almighty's help. Then John surreptitiously flicked an elbow, which was Duncan's sign to send the troops at them.

With a roar, the group of soldiers raced towards them, brandishing pitchforks and dressed in red and black to represent devilish hordes.

"So we cannot meet," John continued, speaking under his breath, "once the masque tomorrow is complete. I am sorry."

Was it his imagination, or did her face fall? Then a steely determination crossed her features. "I am not afraid of the earl," she said, at the same time as she raised her arms to repulse the attackers. She brandished a large bible, which John had 'borrowed' from the chapel.

"He is not someone I want as my enemy." John swung a golden sceptre above his head, which was the cue for the approaching demons to fall and die. "And if he does not trust me, I will not be able to pass on a message about the plot."

"But will they not just attack the king another day?" Margaret raised her arms in victory, then turned to face him. "And not tell you, since they will know who told him of the plot."

That was John's signal to kneel. "The king will have to have a sudden message to visit his father. Or his priest. Something believable—"

Margaret interrupted him with a mirthless chuckle. "Not his priest. None of the lords would believe that." She took the oversized paste and gilt crown from her head and held it towards him.

"His family then. Something that will not implicate us."

She placed the crown on his head, symbolically passing the crown of Scotland from Mary to her son, James. "But the queen will know."

"Mayhap she will imprison the plotters. Or exile them."

"She has done that before, 'tis true."

He stood, and turned with her to face the battleground. "So are we agreed?" He hissed from the side of his mouth. "We cannot meet after tomorrow. Not until I have news of the plot."

Before she could reply, Bastian approached them from the roadway, clapping his hands and shouting up at them. "Bravo, bravo! You have good dramatic instincts, my lord. Adding the bible and sceptre was an inspired touch. It adds to our theme, that our queen is the God-given ruler of this land."

John inclined his head. "'Twas naught."

"You are too modest for an actor in one of my masques. Now," the Frenchman shooed at the soldiers, urging them to get up, "let us away. I must prepare for the feast tonight." He turned and headed back up the road towards the portcullis.

At the other side of the battleground, nearer the castle walls, a shadowy figure stood, staring across at them malignantly. *Bothwell's spy*. It had to be. John clenched his fists. "Let us go down, my lady," he said, ushering her towards the internal ladder. As usual, he went first, then waited for her to hand down their props.

Once everything was stowed in the wooden chest Bastian had provided for the purpose, Margaret descended, with John at the bottom, ready to catch her should she slip.

"Nobody can see us from outside," he whispered up at her. Where he stood was shielded from the open entrance to the tower by one of the supporting columns. "But the earl's man is watching. So we cannot linger."

Hurrying down the last steps, she reached for him. "Then let us make this worthwhile." Suddenly her lips were on his, her hands were in his hair and the scent of vanilla enveloped him, clouding his brain.

For a minute, just a brief minute, he was transported to heaven. He could almost hear the angelic choirs singing and feel the glorious light warming his face. *If this is what dying is like, mayhap I will not mind it.* Her kisses were like an elixir from Elysium.

The clomp of heavy footsteps outside broke them apart. Hastily, Margaret stepped toward the entrance, just as four of the soldiers marched by, making fun of a comrade for his over-exaggerated death throes.

Tugging at his leather jerkin, John picked up his hat and accompanied her back to the castle. They talked little and walked a distance apart, so the watcher would not think there was any closeness between them

But John could still feel the imprint of Margaret's mouth on his lips, and the touch of her fingers on his neck.

These next days were going to be an exquisite torture.

CHAPTER 13

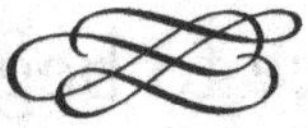

THURSDAY 19TH DECEMBER 1566

From his seat at the round table at the head of the great hall, Bothwell failed to stop his jaw dropping. What fantasy had that Frenchman concocted now?

All eyes were on the decorated trestle as it was pulled into the open area near the doors by servants dressed as nymphs and satyrs, accompanied by musicians dressed as dryads.

Bedecked in green and gold, with real leaves and branches sprouting from its centre, the moving table was groaning under the weight of dishes and plates destined for the baptismal feast.

With a clap of his hands, Bastian Pages signalled for service to begin, and, in a flurry of activity, bowls of creamy Soup à la Reine were placed in front of each distinguished guest. *Queen's Soup. How appropriate.*

Across from him, in pride of place, the queen visibly relaxed as this first course of the meal was distributed. Catching her eye, Bothwell raised his wine goblet in a silent toast, earning him a graceful nod in reply.

The next courses were distributed in similar fashion, with the nymphs and satyrs getting more flamboyant with each portion they served. Bothwell narrowed his eyes and sniffed suspiciously as an elfin-faced faun delivered a platter of meat to his place. *Alcohol! The boy smelled of alcohol!* No wonder the servants were behaving so flippantly. They had been helping themselves to the wine meant for the guests!

Biting back his anger, Bothwell crooked a finger at a valet, and sent him in search of Pages. Testily, he pulled at the embroidered cuffs of his new blue outfit, picked up his knife and speared a particularly juicy piece of beef, imagining that it was the Frenchman he stabbed, not his dinner.

Then he glanced across at Mary, and his mood eased, his ire disappearing as quickly as it had flared. She was looking particularly resplendent this evening in a gown made from cloth of gold and ivory satin. It had not been lost on him that he was wearing a new outfit similar to the ones she had ordered for her half-siblings. And he was seated directly opposite his queen, in the place where the king should have sat.

How lucky for him that the royal wastrel was skulking in his chamber instead of attending his son's baptism. It meant that

Bothwell was one step further in his plan to win the crown, and, if all went well with their Craigmillar plot, perhaps in the near future he would *earn* the right to sit here.

Puffing out his chest, he smirked, congratulating himself on his successes—present and future. He was convinced that Darnley's loss would be his gain.

~

Chewing on a tender slice of veal, Mary surveyed the hall. All seemed to be going well, and Bastian's spectacle appeared to have achieved its aim of awing the lords and dignitaries. "My lord," she addressed the Earl of Bedford, who sat to her right, "have you ever seen such an extravaganza as this?"

"No, ma'am, I do not believe I ever—what!" The English ambassador broke off, staring open mouthed at a group of satyrs, who were dancing and wiggling their tails at him. "What are they doing?" he spluttered. "Do they mock me? I know you Scots jest that we English have tails. But this is unconscionable!"

The veal turned to sawdust in Mary's mouth. Eyes casting desperately around the room, she spotted Bastian talking to Bothwell, and signalled frantically for him. At the same time, she laid a soothing hand on Bedford's arm. "'Tis just a dance, my lord. They are in high spirits."

"Harumph." The ambassador glowered at the servants, who were being ushered away by the Frenchman, still waggling their behinds.

But then another voice piped up from nearby—Sir Christopher Hatton, the English Chancellor, another of the party sent to represent Elizabeth at the baptism. "What are these fools doing? They insult England!" Springing up from his chair, he dragged it across the stage and thumped down with his arms crossed and his back to the spectacle.

Mary stifled a groan. Why had she been so quick to congratulate herself on the success of the meal?

But this time, surprisingly, Lord Bedford came to her aid. Throwing his napkin down on the table, he stomped across to the chancellor, his moustache twitching as he muttered to himself. Mary heard him say something to his countryman about 'insulting their Scottish hosts' and 'over-exuberant servants' and 'the good name of our queen'.

Eventually, Hatton seemed to be won over, and he sheepishly returned to his place, dipping a placatory bow in Mary's direction as he did so.

Mary acknowledged him with a nod of her head, then placed her shaking hands on her lap, lest anyone should see how affected she'd been. At least there was only one more course to go. Surely nothing else could go wrong?

At the side of the great hall, Margaret watched open-mouthed as the English dignitaries showed their offence at the antics of Bastian's satyrs. The queen looked as if she wished the ground would swallow her up, and Margaret's heart twisted for her. It would be awful if the situation stressed Mary's tense relationship with Queen Elizabeth even further.

Then, from across the hall, she saw John rolling his eyes, and she had to smother her laughter with a napkin, before Bothwell's spy would see her. Fortunately, the snooper had been placed at a table lower down the hall and his view of Fincastle was blocked by a particularly large gentleman who sat in the way, his handlebar moustache taking up almost as much room as his wide shoulders.

However, Margaret could be seen by the spy, and she had to be careful not to look in John's direction too often.

"What happens, my lady?" The minor English lord who sat beside her put a hand on her arm, and she had to clench her teeth to stop from shrugging him off. She couldn't tell if he was shortsighted, or just too short to see, but he appeared to be clueless as to the altercations at the head table.

"'Tis just the ambassador. He does not appear to understand the symbolism of Bastian's entertainments. Oh!" Margaret's palm flew to her chest and her eyes raised to the rafters as an angel dressed in white and gold descended from above.

It looked so real, it took her a minute to realise it was a part of the play. *Bravo, Bastian!* What better way to divert the attention of the English dignitaries from the satyr's tails than by producing a spectacle such as this?

The way the heavenly being floated down from the ceiling on a golden orb seemed to defy all understanding. And the words from her mouth were the sweetest verses ever heard, rhyming couplets telling of love, unity and kindness.

All eyes in the room were on the angel, and the servants used that as a cover to roll in the trestle with the final course: the sweetmeats. Butterflies tickled Margaret's throat, for it meant the masque would start soon.

In the central aisle, the satyrs heaved on the ropes to pull the trestle further up the hall, but there were only two on one side and six on the other, and, with a terrible crash, one of the wheels gave way and the table lurched to the ground. Servants ran every which way, rescuing plates and bowls before they slid to the ground, and, at the top table, the queen put her head in her hands.

Margaret jumped to her feet and turned for the door, unable to watch any more. Everything was going wrong, and it augured badly for their masque. What would happen next? Would their tower catch fire? Or would one of the soldiers die for real? She dreaded to think.

And then she spotted John, his shoulder under the edge of the broken trestle to lift it level while a servant tried to fix the buckled wheel.

It was in that moment that Margaret realised she was in love with the laird.

Her legs gave way, and she sat back down again, clutching the edge of the table as if she would surely keel over if she let go. "He is such a kind man," she whispered to herself. "A worthy man."

The English lord gave her a strange look.

She remained still for a minute, blinking,

not caring whether Bothwell's spy could see her, her knees too weak to carry her and her brain reeling in surprise. She—the woman who had once sworn off men, who had remained single all these years while friends around her married and had family—she had finally fallen in love, and it was the strangest feeling.

Even if John did not care for her, she could bear that—she could admire him from afar. It would be hard, especially with the eyes and ears of court watching every move someone made, hunting for gossip to pass the idle hours—but she could do it. She was strong. And proud.

When a naiad appeared at her shoulder with a brimming platter, Margaret waved her away. "I do not think I can eat any more." But it was time to prepare for their masque, and she needed to go. "Excuse me, my lord," she said to the Englishman, straightened her back, and headed for the exit.

CHAPTER 14

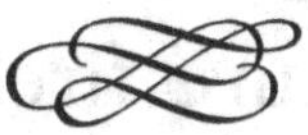

From her pavilion to the southwest of the enchanted fortress, Mary stared in wonder as John and Margaret—dressed in royal robes and representing herself and young James—stood tall and unflinching as they came under attack from a fearsome army.

Under the navy sky with its sprinkling of stars, the tower they stood on glowed magically, needing no illumination because it was surrounded by rings of fire.

Hair flying wild in the wind, soldiers

from her honour guard rampaged towards the mock castle. Dressed in blue and green with horned helmets on their heads, they looked like a troop of barbarous Vikings as they threw miniature fireballs at the castle. But rather than quailing under the assault, the monarchs merely fired a fearsome cannon, and the barbarians fell to the ground as if dead.

The next wave of assailants were costumed in colourful, flowing robes with cloth wrapped around their heads like turbans. Letting forth an eerie yipping sound that made her blood run cold, the infidels brandished their fearsome curved swords and descended on the fortress in a relentless wave of destruction.

But once again, the Queen and her Prince fired their cannon to repulse the invaders, and they, too, were vanquished before they could reach the walls.

Suddenly it all made sense to Mary, and

she clapped her hands in delight at how clever it was. The masque alluded to the history of her kingdom, of how the Stuarts had defeated all their enemies and remained sovereigns over this wild and beautiful land. Beside her, the English and French ambassadors shuffled in their seats. They, too, had seen the allegory.

As the moon rose higher in the night sky, the final attack began, and it was the stuff of Mary's nightmares. A fiendish horde of demons with pointed tails, wreathed in red flames and pointing vicious tridents, screeched like dervishes as they rampaged towards the Scottish royalty.

But cannonballs would surely not defeat such a supernatural enemy? Mary gnawed at a fingernail, her stomach in knots at the thought of the evil forces that massed against her. In the tower, the actors stood passively, their heads bowed and hands clasped as if praying. Mary bounced a knee in agitation. They needed to *do* something. How else could they win?

The players answer was a masterstroke.

For they *had* been doing something, Mary realised. They had been asking for help from the Almighty.

With a flourish, Margaret raised a large bible, and the leading hellions faltered and came to a halt. Then John lifted a golden sceptre into the air, and the devilish army screamed and writhed in agony, falling to the ground and thrashing violently in their death throes.

In the tower, the Prince and Queen clasped hands and raised them in victory.

Mary felt exhausted, like she had been fighting along with them. But she had also learned the lesson she was sure had been the intention of the playwrights. *Trust in God.* Who else was more powerful to help? And how else could a mere woman hope to defeat her enemies, even if she was the rightful queen?

She would be even more devout from now on, Mary decided. 'Twas the only way to win against scheming lords and unfaithful husbands. It would be her motto, emblazoned on her heart. *Trust in God.*

John's heart thudded in his ears as he surveyed the chaotic battlefield before them. Bodies lay everywhere, their discarded weapons glowing evilly in the flickering light from the fire pits. Then, from the castle walls beyond, a trumpet sounded, which was his cue to kneel before Margaret.

Knowing that nobody could hear their words, and aware that this might be his last chance to speak with her privately until the Craigmillar plot was done, he slipped a hand into the pocket of his doublet. "Do nothing," he cautioned, "and keep to our script. But I fear we may not be able to talk much after this, and I wanted to ask you something."

Margaret lifted the crown from her head, and gave the tiniest lift of an eyebrow, something no distant onlooker would spot. "Yes?"

At waist height, so the audience would not see, he held out the ring; Lizzie's ring, that he'd kept safe ever since she died.

His throat dry and his chest tight, he screwed up his courage and blurted out the words. "Marry me, Margaret. Be my wife. I think I've loved ye since the first moment I spied you, and I want to take ye away from all this madness, and back to the safety of Perthshire. With me." Unsure how his declaration would be received, he held his breath.

Reaching across with the crown, Margaret faltered momentarily, and there was a gasp from the crowd. But she covered up the stumble, adding an extra theatrical flourish as she placed the crown on his head. At the same time, she ducked her face and whispered, "Yes, I will marry you. I love you too, Laird Fincastle, although it was only this evening I came to realise it."

It took all John's willpower not to leap up and embrace her. Instead, he murmured, "I want to kiss ye. But it will have to wait, I'm afraid." Standing, he took her hand, pressing the ring into it. Then they turned together to face their audience, bowing from the waist as cheers and applause erupted from around the field.

Almost tripping in their haste to descend from the tower so they could be alone, however briefly, they fell into each other's arms at the bottom of the stair. "I cannot wear the ring openly lest Bothwell see it," Margaret murmured between kisses, "but I will put it on a chain and carry it next to my heart."

"Aye," John agreed, his chest almost bursting with happiness.

"But I have an idea how we can meet."

"You do?" John pushed her away from him, frowning.

"Yes. Take one of the hairpieces from the Vikings, and a tunic from the Moors. In the darkness, you will pass for a woman. Then you can meet me in the sewing room of an evening. After dinner, perhaps."

His mind whirling, John stared at her. "Aye," he said slowly, "it might work. Nine of the clock, each night?"

"Be sure to give Bothwell's man the slip first."

"I could send Duncan out for a walk, dressed in my cloak?"

She nodded. "That might work." Then an explosion rocked the night, and she looked anxiously at the doorway. "The fireworks. They are starting."

"Aye. We need to be quick." After one last kiss, he took the fake crown from his head and began to root through the box of props, balling a black wig inside a green robe and buttoning them inside his doublet.

"You look like you partook of too many sweetmeats at the feast!" Margaret poked at his fake paunch.

"Aye, but with my cloak on," he swept the woollen mantle around his shoulders, "no-one will be able to tell."

"Better," she said, and smiled up at him as another bang sounded from the battlements. "Come, I want to see these fireworks. I have never seen such a thing before."

"Nobody has, I hear tell. 'Tis the first time in Scotland."

"Even more reason to hurry," she said, and then she was gone out of the door.

John stood for a moment, gazing at the space where she'd been, a smile playing on his lips. *My wife-to-be.* He could not believe that he would be so lucky for a second time, to find another fascinating woman who loved him. And it would fulfil the terms of his inheritance. *Although I would have married her regardless.*

But then another blast rent the air, reminding him of the pledge he'd made to the other nobles. *If I live long enough to wed her, that is.* With a shiver, he threw the folds of the cloak around his shoulder, and hurried outside to watch the spectacle, hoping that these explosions would be the last he'd hear for some long time.

~

As the last massive bang rent the sky, and sparks of light burst in a cloud like the sun, Bothwell looked along the line of dignitaries seated in the pavilion, and spotted the queen. Her face was entranced, hands clasped under her throat, cheeks flushed and eyes sparkling.

In that moment, she looked like a young girl, and Bothwell almost felt guilty that he, who had seen his thirty third birthday earlier this year, had designs on her.

But then he remembered that she was his route to the throne, and he pushed those feelings behind him.

Now the baptism was over, Moray, Maitland and the others could begin to think about their plot against the king once more.

With the completion of the firework display, the queen sprang to her feet and began clapping enthusiastically, sparking a wave of applause that echoed across the field.

Bothwell used that as his cover to slip away, finding his man, Nicholas Hubert, known as 'French Paris', lurking behind the tent. "Well? Did you find any evidence that they are in league?"

Paris shook his head. "No, sire, not yet. But it was hard to tell what went on in the tower."

"Nothing much, I should think, with the eyes of half of Scotland upon them. Nevertheless, you should continue your vigilance. Mayhap now that the masque is done, they will let their guard down."

"Yes, sire."

Bothwell made a shooing motion. "Let us away. 'Tis time for the investiture of young James as Prince of Scotland. I must attend."

On the walk back up to the castle, by fortuitous chance he happened to fall in alongside the Highlander, Laird Fincastle.

Grudgingly, he felt compelled to congratulate the laird for his part in the masque. But then he quickly moved on to the subject that was uppermost in his mind. "Think you, Fincastle, that we might, ah, move forward with our plan, here at Stirling?"

The laird gave him a sideways glance. "Here, with the queen and all the foreign dignitaries around every corner?"

"Yes. The king has his apartment separately to Mary, does he not?"

"But—" here the Highlander seemed to

search for the right words to use, ones that would seem innocent if they were overheard, "my tools are not very precise. 'Tis hard to tell of their effect, and how far-reaching it might be."

Bothwell clenched his teeth, swearing under his breath. "So we must wait, then."

"Aye. There will be better opportunity soon, I am sure."

Giving his companion a measured look, Bothwell noted the readiness with which he'd offered that last opinion. *Mayhap he is with us after all. Perhaps I was wrong to doubt him.*

But then his natural caution took hold again. 'Twould still be wise to have Paris spy on him. *Just in case.*

Kingdoms had been lost for less.

CHAPTER 15

Seated behind the queen in the royal chapel, Margaret craned her neck to see if she could spot the laird. He had said he would be there, when they'd met in the little sewing room last night, but he was nowhere to be seen.

She also couldn't see Bothwell's man, Paris, which at least meant that he also would not be able to observe her.

How he had not spotted their subterfuge each evening, she would never know. When

Duncan, disguised as Fincastle, would head for the battlements, he would always follow, leaving the coast clear for Margaret and John to meet, albeit briefly.

They treated each night as if it were their last together, at least until the plotters had been uncovered, and made the most of every minute they had.

Sharing stories of their youth and discussing the people that surrounded them in the castle, they found they had a very similar approach to life, and were in agreement with their hopes for the future. And, of course, they shared embraces too. But they were, of necessity, fleeting moments, in case anyone should enter the room and discover them.

As Mary Fleming processed down the aisle in her dress of satin and silk on the arm of her brother John, the current Lord Fleming, Margaret finally spotted the laird, who had slipped into a pew near the back. He caught her eye, and winked at her, before turning to the front, his handsome face a picture of innocence.

Watching the beautiful lady-in-waiting as she married old Maitland, the queen's secretary who had somehow captured her heart, Margaret found herself dreaming of her own wedding.

At least things were moving forward on that front. Now that the queen had pardoned Lord Morton for his part in the murder of Riccio, Bothwell had set up a meeting for mid-January to appraise him of the plot, and invited John along.

Perhaps at that meeting the conspirators would decide on a date, and then she and John could warn the queen, and save the king's life.

'Twould not be long, she was sure of it, and then she, too, would be wed.

With a contented sigh, she sat back in her

chair and watched avidly as the bride and her groom traded words, and made their pledges, imagining herself and John in their place.

A smile played on her lips. She would sleep well that night for sure, with such pleasant inspiration for her dreams.

~

"A favour, you say?" Mary sat by the fire in her ante-chamber, a piece of embroidery on her lap.

"Yes, ma'am," Bothwell said, "but not an onerous one, I hope."

The queen motioned to a stool nearby. "Sit, my lord, and tell me what you need."

Settling himself on the tapestry-clad chair, Bothwell gazed briefly around the sumptuous apartment, then rested his elbows on his knees and stared earnestly across at her. "My queen, you know my man, Paris?"

"Yes. Nicholas Hubert."

"The very one. If you are agreeable, I would wish for him to enter your service. He needs polish, and I am sure that some months as a part of your household would do that for him."

"But," Mary frowned, "do you not need him with you?"

Yes, Bothwell thought, but his mouth said otherwise. "I can manage without him. He will be a better servant at the end of it."

Mary lifted a shoulder, in that elegant French way. "Very well. Have him attend in my rooms tomorrow morning."

"Thank you, ma'am." Bothwell hid a smile. With Paris in place, he would more easily be able to spy on the laird and the lady Carwood. Just in case the laird was not as loyal as he appeared. For the earl was a careful man, and he would not have his plot unmasked, not at this late stage.

"Have you heard anything of the king, my lord?"

Mary's question took him by surprise. "I hear he is very unwell, and that his hair has fallen out." He could not resist sharing that juicy tidbit. "But because he is sick, he has not been able to sail for Europe."

"Did he really think he was in danger here? I cannot believe he would leave us."

"Mayhap the illness scrambled his thinking. But I imagine he worried he would be arrested for his part in the killing of Riccio, and charged with treason. So he left for the safety of his father's estates in Glasgow."

Her expression sad, the queen shook her head. "Does he not think that I would have imprisoned him long ago, should I mean to?"

"'Tis likely he judges you by his own standards, and does not realise how kind you are."

Mary's face brightened at his praise, and then clouded again. "Who would have guessed that marriage could be so difficult. It is supposed to be a joyous union."

"Quite so, ma'am," Bothwell replied, hiding his surprise at her candour. He knew she sometimes confided in Maitland, but this was the first confidence that she had shared with him. Her trust in him must really be growing.

"But of course, you would know that. It is not so long since you married your Jean."

"As you say, ma'am." He dropped his head, lest she see his expression. His own marriage seemed to fare best when he and Jean were living in different places.

"I shall remember Darnley in my prayers, Lord Bothwell. I am sure he will recover soon, and join me again here in Stirling before we return to Edinburgh."

What was it Maitland had said the other day? *You might conclude such a thing. I could not possibly guess at the king's motivations.* One day he would be secure enough in his position to say that out loud, but for now he merely repeated his previous words. "As you say, ma'am."

CHAPTER 16

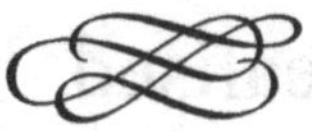

MONDAY 20TH JANUARY 1567

Mary moved to the window of her tapestried drawing room, pushed aside the heavy drapes, and gazed over the parkland adjacent to Holyrood Palace, her vision swimming. "I cannot believe it, Monsieur du Croc. The king is unwell. How could he think to do such a thing?"

The French ambassador smoothed his pointed beard. "I must apologise, Ma'am, but it is what I heard, and I thought you would wish to know. The king plans to kidnap the prince from Stirling, stage a coronation, and then govern as regent."

She rounded on him. "But what about me?" Then she realised how petulant that sounded. "I am queen. How does he think to rule when I am the rightful monarch?"

"He believes the Protestant lords are in support of him, rather than you. That they will force you to abdicate, then imprison you." A shoulder lifted eloquently. "I am sorry to say."

Mary wanted to throw something. Or tear something to pieces. Or scream at the top of her voice. But she was queen, and she could not let this foreign dignitary see her lose her temper, well-disposed toward her as he was. Instead, she strode to the door, and threw it open. "Wine," she commanded the page who waited in the corridor. "For two. As quickly as you can."

The door was too heavy to slam—perhaps just as well—so she paced to the other end of the room, and adjusted a candlestick on the mantelpiece, then moved to a dresser and tweaked the leaves of a flower arrangement, before returning to the window and leaning on the sill, her breathing ragged.

"If I may suggest, ma'am, an ancient Chinese general said that the supreme art of war is to subdue the enemy without fighting."

Mary had no idea what he was implying, but she was saved from answering by the arrival of the page with a bottle of claret and two goblets.

The alcohol burned its way down her throat and churned in her stomach, but somehow it managed to soothe her.

Du Croc picked up his wine and sniffed at the red liquid before taking a tentative sip. "What I mean to say is, if you can persuade the king to return to Edinburgh, you can try to win him over with your charms."

"Tempt him with the crown matrimonial, you mean, like I did at Stirling?"

"You may not even need to do that. I hear he is disfigured with the pox, so he may be susceptible to your—ah, womanly allure, if you should appear favourable towards him."

"And if he is here in Holyrood, I suppose I will know better who he is seeing and what he is doing."

"Exactement."

Mary nodded. And then she frowned. "But I do not want him *here*," she raised an arm to indicate the palace, "lest we see a repeat of the night poor David was murdered."

Despite his repentance and their seeming reconciliation, Mary had never been fully able to forgive her husband and the group of Scottish nobles who had conspired against— and murdered—her secretary and friend, David Riccio.

She understood that Darnley had been jealous, and that jealousy could turn a man insane, but *knowing* something was not proving sufficient to change her feelings. It had been an unspeakable thing that they did. "I will get Bothwell to prepare some rooms for him at Craigmillar, where he can recover in privacy but we can be informed of his actions."

"That sounds wise."

"And I will go now to Glasgow and persuade him to return with me." She slammed her palm on the table. "This very afternoon, before he conspires any further against me."

The ambassador raised his glass in a toast. "Bonne chance, ma'am. Bonne chance."

Good luck, he says?

She would need it.

John paced towards the men sheltering under a huge yew tree in the grounds of Whittinghame Tower in East Lothian, hoping his face didn't show the anxiety he felt inside. It would not be politic to look nervous in front of these men.

"Good morrow, my lords," he said when he reached them, bowing politely.

"Laird Fincastle," Maitland inclined his head in greeting. "You will not have met James Douglas, the Earl of Morton, who owns this place." He indicated a red-bearded man in a tall hat.

"I do not see how we can do this," Morton said, launching straight into business. "I am only just returned from exile. If the queen does not agree with it, I could find myself back in England again." He almost spat the word.

"She will agree, once 'tis done," said Maitland. "She told me herself, in Jedburgh, that she considered Darnley most unsuitable as a king. But we cannot tell her beforehand. She must not know of what we plan."

"Bothwell says you contemplate an explosion?" Morton looked sceptical.

"Yes. This is where Fincastle will aid us." Maitland pointed at John, obviously expecting him to speak.

"I can supply gunpowder, from my quarry in Perthshire."

Bothwell slapped his gloves against his palm. "Send for it now. This very day, the queen goes to Glasgow to retrieve the king. If she gets her way, he will be in Craigmillar before the week is out. We must get the powder stowed below his chambers in the castle before he arrives."

"'Tis fortunate, then, that I have a shipment arriving tomorrow at Leith. I shall away and ready a cart." John said, looking from one to the other, hardly able to believe that this was really happening, "And deliver it to Craigmillar Castle."

The earl took a step towards him. "I shall

meet you there tomorrow and oversee the unloading."

"'Twill be evening at the earliest. The boat is not due at the docks till midday and then we need to load the oxen" He did a quick calculation. "Mayhap five of the clock afore we reach the castle. 'Tis not safe to travel fast with powder. But 'twill be dark by then."

"All the better to hide your destination." Bothwell's eyes bored into his. "Be as quick as you can. I shall be waiting."

~

Darnley banged his fist on the mattress. "I will not go to Craigmillar. Simon Fraser hates me. And I do not trust the earl to prepare me rooms there. I think he means me ill." In the oversized bed in his father's house in Glasgow, wearing a white nightshirt with ruffles made from linen she'd sent over, he looked like a petulant child.

Mary clenched her teeth, battening down her frustration before she replied, "Well, you may join me at Holyrood instead. 'Twas only consideration for your recuperation which had me think you'd prefer somewhere quieter. But we can reconcile at Holyrood just as well."

"No, not the palace either. How can I have people seeing me like this?" He indicated his pock-marked face, which was covered in red weals.

She had forgotten about his vanity. "I can ask the ambassador to let Doctor Nau attend you—you will have heard of his good reputation."

"I may have. But I heard he has some strange ideas."

"Mayhap his cures seem unusual. But they seem to work. Now, if you will not stay at Craigmillar or Holyrood, is there some-where else nearby we could consider?"

"Mayhap." He scratched his chin thought-fully. "Robert Balfour owes me a debt from our last game. And he has a house at Kirk o' Field. I shall tell him to accommodate me there."

"Very well," Mary inclined her head. "I shall have your bed and your things sent there. We can leave this afternoon."

"But everything may not be ready for my arrival," he whined.

It took all her willpower not to roll her eyes at his infantile attitude. "In the morning, then. Immediately after we break our fast."

The next day, accompanying a rumbling oxen cart shrouded in miz-zling rain and mist, John spent the long hours on the road from Leith trying to work out whether that last statement of the earl's was meant as a promise—or a threat.

Saddlesore and weary, wishing he'd not left Duncan up in Perthshire so he wouldn't have had to accompany the wagon himself, they were passing through Kamron when a rider cantered up alongside and hailed him. "John Stewart of Tulliepowries?"

"Aye. Who asks?"

"I've a message from the Earl of Bothwell. He says your destination is no longer Craigmillar, but a house in Edinburgh. I've to accompany you to the Cowgate Port, and he will meet us there."

Bothwell's man was a morose Borderer with a fulsome moustache set over an unsmiling mouth. In the hour it took them to return to the city, he said little, apart from a few grunts to his garron. And the carter was a no better.

Thus John was left to gaze at the damp countryside that surrounded them, and worry about whether he had been taken for a fool, and was even now being double-crossed. What perplexed him most was the location of the king. If he was not at Craigmillar, then where *was* he? Surely the conspirators would not consider blowing up the palace? So where was the gunpowder to go?

He got his answer when the earl met them at the city gate, and led them to a house on a narrow lane off the Cowgate. Tall buildings on either side crowded towards them as if wanting to be a part of the plot.

Bothwell directed the servants to start unloading, then drew John aside. "We will store the barrels here in Morton's house for now," he said, jerking his chin at the basement. "That fool Darnley refused to stay at Craigmillar, and has said that instead he'll go to the old Blackfriars Monastery at Kirk o' Field. But 'twould be foolish to move until we are certain of his location."

Once the powder barrels were stacked

below Morton House, the carter tipped his hat at the laird, tucked his fee into his jerkin, and led his oxen off up the street. It was only then that John thought about where he would sleep for the night.

On his previous visit to Edinburgh, he'd been a guest at the palace. But he couldn't presume to stay there now, unless… Perhaps Margaret would be able to organise a room for him. But how would he get in touch with her? He scratched his head, realising that his only option was to turn up at the gates and ask. Otherwise it was a boarding house and a lumpy paillasse for him…

Unhitching Dirk, he was turning the horse towards the High Street when Bothwell appeared at the door. "There's a room for you here, should you wish," the earl said. "Your horse can go in the stables." He jerked his head at a pend on the right.

John stood indecisively for a moment, weighing up the likelihood of being spied on at the palace against the certainty of being watched at Morton's house. "Thank ye," he said, unbuckling his saddlebag and throwing it over his shoulder.

Being here under Bothwell's nose would be excruciating. But mayhap it would convince the earl of his good intentions, of his genuine involvement in the plot. In turn, that might actually mean he was snooped on less, and it would be easier to warn the king when the time came.

Of course, the fact that an easement in being watched over might also make it easier for him to meet with Margaret had no bearing at all on his decision…

Margaret stared at the book in her hand, realising that she'd read the same words over and over again, and still hadn't taken in their meaning.

With the queen over in Glasgow, visiting with Darnley, there was little to do here in the palace of Holyrood. But that meant her mind had time to wander, and to worry about John and their inadvertent part in the plot against the king.

It had been over a week since she'd seen him, since the queen's party had left Stirling.

Instead of travelling to Edinburgh, he had decided to return to his estates in Perthshire and organise the gunpowder he'd offered to the plotters. It seemed the lords still meant to go ahead with their plans.

"My lady," a voice at her shoulder startled her, and she looked up into the mousy face and dark eyes of Bothwell's spy, Nicholas Hubert.

Much to Margaret's alarm, although she could say nothing to her mistress, Bothwell had persuaded the queen to take Paris into her household. So now Margaret could be spied on, night and day—except there was nothing to see, of course, with the laird returned home.

It had been a different situation at Stirling. Somehow, the disguise with the wig and robe had worked, and Margaret had been able to meet with John on a regular basis in the sewing room.

They had talked of the past, and of the future they hoped to share together, of the children they would have, God willing, and the years that they would share. Her heart swelled to think on it.

But that future could not happen until the plot was uncovered and the king was safe.

"Paris," Margaret replied, her voice cold, "what is it you want?" He was not in the habit of talking to her—in fact, they had never conversed—and she could not imagine what he wanted of her now.

"I wonder if you could take a turn with me around the gardens. I'm told you know of the herbs and medicinal plants, and I wish to learn of them."

"Can you not see that I am busy here?"

With an arch of his eyebrow, Paris glanced at her book, and then back at her face. "So busy reading that you cannot spare a few minutes to help a new member of the household?"

"But there is nothing of note to see in winter. 'Tis better to visit the gardens in spring."

"Even so, I would wish to learn of what there is to know. January cannot be entirely barren, surely?"

With a theatrical sigh, Margaret placed her book face-down on the window seat, hoping he would get the hint that she intended to return to it. "Very well, let us go to the kitchen garden."

But when they reached the walled enclosure where the gardeners grew the produce that helped keep the royal larders full, it became obvious that Paris had no real interest in the plants. Instead, he seemed more interested in Margaret.

"How long is it you have worked for the queen?" he asked, trailing his hand along the fragrant lavender bushes that lined the path, releasing their summery aroma.

"Three years this spring." She pointed at the grey-leaved shrub under his hand. "Lavender is good for pains of the heart, for rousing one who faints, and to help with a sound sleep."

"And do you always take part in the masques organised by Monsieur Pages?"

"If I am asked, yes."

"And what about the Highlander, Laird Fincastle?" He gave her a sharp look as he asked this.

"He acted in the masque at Craigmillar, and the one at Stirling, which I believe you saw." She gave him her own sideways glance. "But I understand he has returned to his estates." She shrugged, affecting a disinterested air. "I doubt we will see him again. Now, this—" she indicated a larger shrub behind the lavender, "is rosemary. It can be burned against black plague, or you can soak your feet in an infusion to help with gout.

"Yes, yes. So when did you meet Fincastle?"

"When he arrived at Craigmillar." She stopped and put her hands on her hips. "Why do you ask?"

"Oh, no reason." He put his hands in his pockets and scuffed the toe of his boot on the path. But her retaliation seemed to take the wind out of his sails, and from then on he attended better to her comments about the plants, even asking a few relevant questions. Finally, he remarked, "Monsieur Nau used herbs to help the queen when she was sick at Jedburgh. And also my master, who had suffered a sword wound."

"I have heard that the doctor is very skilled."

"I would like to be like him. To heal people."

Margaret blinked in surprise. This was not what she had expected of Bothwell's spy.

The next three afternoons, Paris sought her out, and persuaded her to go walking in the gardens again. With the queen still in Glasgow and nothing better to do, she accepted. But on Friday, as they exited from the vaulted kitchen, he took her arm and pulled her closer to him.

Suddenly, his motives became clear. *He is trying to form an attachment with me.* Probably he hoped to use that against the laird, when John eventually returned to Edinburgh.

Clutching at her stomach, Margaret hunched forward, groaning loudly.

"What is it?" Paris' face blanched. "Is it poison?"

Margaret had heard the rumours of

Mary's poisoning in Jedburgh, and could understand why he might think that. "No," she gasped, hamming it up, "'tis my—my monthly…" then she shook her head, hiding her face from him as if ashamed, "I cannot talk about it. I must go!"

Turning away from him, she hurried back into the palace and up to her room. Hopefully, if he thought she had her monthly courses, he would avoid her for a few days. By then the queen ought to be back, and Margaret could be 'too busy' to walk with him.

Staring out of the small window in her turret room, she gazed at the northern sky. Somewhere up there, miles away, where eagles soared and the hills rolled into the distance like waves on the sea, was John. Her heart yearned for his company, and to hear the melodious rumble of his voice. And yet, when she next saw him, it would mean the plot was nearing its conclusion, and he would be in danger.

With a sigh, Margaret lay down on her narrow bed, her insides hurting for real this time. All she could do was to ask that God would keep John safe until they could be together again. Closing her eyes, she quieted her mind and began to pray.

CHAPTER 17

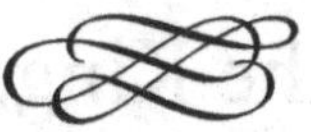

SUNDAY 26TH JANUARY 1567

As the priest intoned the words of his final blessing, Mary mused on the theme of his homily, where he'd spoken of the acts of charity and mercy that could be carried out by ordinary people. Back in Stirling, she'd vowed to place her trust in God, and now here she was in the chapel at Holyrood, hearing a message of forgiveness and compassion.

It spoke to her heart, and to the issues she'd been having with her husband. *I should be kinder to him.* Perhaps, like the prodigal son, he would repent of his wanton ways and become a partner she could be proud of, if only she would show him a good example.

"I should visit the King," she whispered to Margaret, who sat beside her. "Bring him alms. Read to him, keep him company. Show him charity."

"Yes, ma'am. The priest did say we should be kind, even to the undeserving."

Mary looked sideways at her lady. Was she talking of the king, or just in general? "We will visit with him tonight, and you shall attend me. Pray that he will be receptive."

Laughter echoed into the room on the upper floor of the Old Provost's Lodging at Kirk o' Field where Margaret and the other ladies sat with Bastian Pages and Nicholas Hubert, waiting for the queen to be finished with her visit to Darnley in the chamber next door.

The house was substantial, on two floors plus a cellar, with a pitched slate roof. Expensive tapestries confiscated from Mary's enemies decorated the king's room, and he could recline in a sumptuous four-poster bed swathed in violet velvet and embellished with cloth of silver and gold.

The ante room, where they sat, was more spartan, as it was only meant to house the sovereign's personal servants.

"Methinks they play Primero," said Bastian. "I wonder who will win?"

Mary Seton shook her head. "No, 'twill be Piquet since there are but two of them."

"The queen will let Darnley win. Otherwise he will grumble." Finishing the leaf she'd been embroidering, Margaret cut the thread, and examined the design. "This will be good for the centrepiece at your wedding, Bastian?" She held it up so he could see.

"Bien, oui. It is very pretty. Merci."

"'Tis but two weeks now till you marry Christy, is it not?" Mary Seton said, her voice quiet and precise.

Bastian gave a theatrical groan. "Oui. It seems a long time to wait, and yet it comes too quickly. There is much still to do."

Margaret's fingers stilled. When would she be able to plan her wedding to John? It was so difficult, with this plot hanging over them and Bothwell's spy watching her every move. And yet she had to help Bastian to get ready for his nuptials in the near future, all the while wishing that it was her *own* wedding she prepared for.

"I will help with the flowers, nearer the time," Mary Seton volunteered.

"Merci. That will be good."

Then the door swung open and the queen exited Darnley's room, a smile on her face. "Paris," she addressed the Frenchman, "Will you arrange for my purple velvet chair to be sent here tomorrow? The one in there has lumps in it that will give me bruises if I sit any longer. And the Turkish carpet from my privy chamber will stop the draughts."

The valet, who had been sitting quietly in the corner, gave a bow. "Of course, ma'am."

"Now, Margaret," Mary caught her arm and led her towards the door, "walk with me, back to the palace."

A few minutes later, they were out in the street, a gay torchlit procession heading down Blackfriars Wynd towards Holyrood.

"My dear Margaret," Mary began, "I hear gossip that you have been spending time with Monsieur Hubert. Are you and Paris becoming attached? I will be sorry to lose you, but it would be good to see you happy."

"No, ma'am, 'tis nothing like that. He has been asking me about garden herbs. I believe he wants to learn about the properties of plants."

Mary looked at Margaret from the

corner of her eye. "But he is handsome, no? Mayhap a trifle short, but…"

"I can't say I noticed, ma'am. Besides—" Then she stopped herself. She'd been about to admit her feelings for John.

"I knew it!" Mary clapped her hands. "You are not interested in Paris. You're in love with the laird!"

"I—" Wrestling with her conscience, Margaret glanced behind them to see if they would be overheard. "I don't know what to say, ma'am." She couldn't bring herself to lie about her feelings, on the Sabbath, of all days. But it was not safe for her to talk about John, not with Bothwell's spy so close at hand.

"'Tis not like you to be lost for words. Have I guessed your secret?" Mary's eyes widened. "Yes! You blush. I do believe I have."

"Ma'am, please, Bastian is to be married in two weeks. We should concentrate on his nuptials. I do not wish to detract from his celebration."

The queen was silent for a few strides. Then she took Margaret's hand, and looked her in the eye. "Has Fincastle proposed to you?"

She must have read the answer in Margaret's expression, because a broad smile lit her face, causing her cheeks to dimple. "He has! I am so happy for you, dear Margaret, the two of you make such a handsome couple. I have thought so since I saw you with him at the masque in Craigmillar."

"But ma'am, we cannot… We cannot be married. It would not be fair to Bastian."

Mary frowned. "Do I understand correctly? You don't want to get married for fear of devaluing Bastian's wedding?"

Taking a deep breath to calm her spinning brain, Margaret tried to work out what to say that would turn the queen from this topic of conversation. "Yes. T'would not be fair."

Her mistress was quiet for a brief spell, then she clapped her hands again. "I have it! 'Tis no harder to organise two weddings than one. We will order double of everything, and you can be married the day after Bastian and Christy. We will keep it a secret from all but the priest until after they are wed."

"The next day? But—"

"You are right. If there is wine, there will be sore heads." Mary touched a finger to her lips. "Two days later, then. That will give the kitchens more time to prepare a second feast. You must tell Laird Fincastle, and I will alert the priest. Bastian will marry on the Sunday, and you will wed your sweetheart on the Tuesday. It will be a week of weddings, no?"

Margaret's head reeled as they passed through the Netherbow Port and onto the

Canongate. *I am to be wed in two weeks!* But how would that sit with the laird, and what would happen about the plot against the king?

It was almost midnight the following day when John finally spotted the little torchlit procession making its way down the hill towards him. He stayed hidden under the overhang of the Cowgate Port until they got close enough for him to be sure that the earl and Paris were not with them. Then he slipped out of the shadows and fell in alongside Margaret. "Good evening, my lady."

Margaret gasped in surprise, and then her face brightened. "'Tis you!" The rest of her party were so engrossed in conversation, they seemed not to have noticed that another had joined their ranks.

"Yes. I am staying at Lord Morton's

house, as you may have heard, and so is Bothwell. So 'twill be difficult to see you, I'm afraid. But I managed to slip out undetected tonight." Thinking that Fincastle was a man with similar proclivities to himself, Bothwell had not questioned his lie that he was away to visit a brothel.

"'Tis wonderful to see you, and I have so much to tell you. But first," her brow knitted, and she checked that her companions were not listening before she continued, "is there anything you need me to tell the queen?"

"Not today. Word reached us that the queen will sleep over at the Provost's House, so nothing can be done until that changes. 'Twould not be safe for her."

"She is not there during the day."

He shook his head. "Too many people would see what we did. So we wait for a better opportunity."

"We?"

How had it suddenly become 'we'? Rubbing the back of his neck, he grimaced. "'Tis hard, living in that house and trying to make them believe I am a part of it."

She swallowed. "I understand. I am glad 'tis not me."

"You said you had news for me?" It seemed politic to change the subject.

"Yes. I'm afraid, the queen has guessed about…" again, she made sure they were not overheard before carrying on, "our future plans."

He raised an eyebrow, but said nothing, sensing that there was more to come.

"So she is planning for us to be married two days after Bastian, on the eleventh. She said it is as easy to organise two weddings as one. But I asked her to keep it secret. I said I didn't want to detract from Bastian's celebrations."

Lifting a shoulder, he made a wry face. "What's done is done. We will just have to pray that things have come to a conclusion with the lords and their plans by then." He did a quick calculation. "We have two weeks."

"Yes." She glanced across at him. "Not long."

They were approaching the palace now, and he was aware that they only had a minute or two before he would have to leave her. "I will come to you again like this," he said hurriedly, "if I can. But if Paris or Bothwell are in your party I will not be able to speak."

She nodded. "We are lucky. The queen asked for Paris to stay over at Blackfriars tonight."

"And I am glad. It has lifted my spirits to see you, even though briefly." He wanted so much to embrace her, but instead had to make do with a brief touch on her arm. "The lords have been invited to Bastian's wedding party, so I shall see you there at the very least."

"I shall look forward to it." Her face glowed. "And to ours."

Onlookers be damned, he thought, and quickly raised her hand to his lips. "I love you," he whispered, and kissed her knuckles, before turning and disappearing into the shadows once more.

In two weeks, this hateful subterfuge would be over—one way or another—and their love would be concealed no longer. He could not wait.

CHAPTER 18

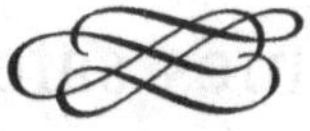

SUNDAY 9TH FEBRUARY 1567

As Mary progressed out of the chapel after morning mass, her half-brother, the Earl of Moray, approached her, looking agitated.

"What ails you, my lord? You look like you sat on a hedgehog."

"'Tis my wife, Your Grace. I have received word that she has lost the baby. I apologise, but I feel I must go to her."

Mary's shoulders sagged. "Of course you must! Poor Agnes. Please give the countess my best wishes, and tell her I shall say a rosary for the bairn." Mary could not imagine what it must be like to miscarry a child, and she thanked God daily for bringing young James safely into the world. She would have been bereft without him.

Moray bent at the waist, his long, sharp nose looking like it would almost peck the ground. "Thank you, ma'am. I will away. My apologies for any privy council meetings I may miss." Then he strode off towards the stables without a backward glance.

Doctor Nau was the next to approach her. He swept his hat off and bowed, his dark hair streaked with chestnut and glistening in the winter sunshine.

"Bonjour, Doctor. How are you this fine morning?"

"Bonjour, Your Grace. I am well, thank you."

"Walk with me," she commanded,

pointing the way, "and tell me, how is the king today?"

"That is why I wanted to speak with you, ma'am. I am pleased to say that the treatment seems to have worked. Or perhaps the country air at Kirk o' Field has been good for him. Whatever," he raised his palm, "I can do no more for him at this point. He is re-covered."

Mary's heart lightened and she almost skipped for a couple of steps. "Bien! Merci beaucoup, Monsieur Nau." These last days and weeks with Darnley had been good. She had actually enjoyed her visits with him, even though they had initially started as a work of charity.

For his part, the disfigurements caused by his mercury treatment had caused the king to stay housebound, rather than carousing in the taverns and whorehouses of Edinburgh as had been his habit.

It had kept him sober, and made him a

more genial companion. He had almost become the man she thought she had married; the dream she had painted in her mind of the tall, handsome lord who would stay by her side and support her as she ruled her kingdom.

And now he was well again! Would he stay by her side this time? *There is only one way to know.*

Beckoning at a page, she gave him a message to take to Kirk o' Field. "Tell the king we will dine with him tonight, and then I shall attend Bastian's wedding party. On the morrow, arrange for his bed and things to be transported back to the palace, and tell him I will look forward to his return. We can have luncheon together in my chamber."

Tomorrow would start a new phase in her life.

Either the king would finally be with her, heart and soul, or, now healed, he would return to his old ways, and she would have to speak to Maitland about divorce and a dispensation from the pope.

But she was decided. She would have the husband she deserved, or she would have none. There was no other way.

Eyes gleaming, Bothwell slapped his cards on the table. "Supremus! I win." Reaching across the table, he made to take the pot.

"I think not." Darnley shook his head primly and fanned out his four cards for all to see. "Primero. *I* win."

Before Bothwell could accuse the blackguard of cheating, Mary took a sip from her wine glass and smiled across the table at the king. "Well done, my husband, you have bested us all."

In that moment, a fire burned in Bothwell's chest, and he hated Darnley more than he ever had before. Just when he had wangled his way into the queen's good graces and was in prime position to take her heart, that knave had to turn over a new leaf and start behaving like a choirboy.

But I will have my revenge. In his rage, Bothwell had almost forgotten the stack of barrels destined for the cellar of the Old Provost's House.

The queen's announcement that the king was recovered and would be returning to Holyrood tomorrow had given the conspirators an immutable deadline. Of course, as usual, the bastard Moray had found a convenient excuse to leave Edinburgh, disassociating himself from their plot, as was his wont.

But that left Bothwell in charge, and he meant to see it was done, and done properly. Moray would get his comeuppance later—when Bothwell was king.

It would have been easier, and they could

have done the deed much sooner, if Mary had not taken to sleeping in the lower room at House o' Field, to save her walking back in the dark. It had meant that they could not attack the king without also endangering the queen. But tonight was their chance. Mayhap their only chance.

Mary stood, and smoothed her skirts. "It is time, I must depart. Bastian and Christy await. We must go." Briefly, she touched her husband's fingers. "Henry, I shall see you tomorrow. Sleep well!"

Sleep well, indeed, my king. Bothwell almost rubbed his hands together. With Mary at the wedding of that coxcomb, Pages, the king would be alone, and he would be at their mercy.

Darnley's valet, William Taylor, held the door open for them as they filed out of the king's room and through the chamber beyond, where the servants waited. There was a scraping of chairs as they jumped to their feet and began gathering their things.

Bothwell signalled to Paris, who fell into step beside him. "Wait half an hour," he whispered, "till they are snoring, then start moving the barrels. I will return with Fincastle to set the charge."

It would not be long now.

The king would be gone, and the queen would be left alone in this world, in need of a strong man to protect her against her foes. And who had done that job countless times already? He smirked to himself.

With a swagger, Bothwell settled his hat on his head and followed the rest of the party to Holyrood. *Not long now.*

"Fincastle, there you are."

The earl of Bothwell strode towards John, who was standing in the dining room off the great hall, eating a plate of cold meats from the array on the table by the wall.

"I have just come from the Rector's house with the queen. The king is there. Alone." Bothwell dipped his head to emphasise this last word. "Finally, we can make our move. I have left Paris in charge of moving the—ah— goods. But we will need you to come and set things up for us."

John frowned. "Set things up?"

The earl glanced around them to be sure they were not overheard. "The fuse," he whispered.

"Ah." John nodded his head slowly. "Of course." Thankful for the acting lessons he'd had from Bastian, he kept his face neutral. But his heart rate had increased, and he was finding it hard to get air into his lungs. The time was now, and he had not yet been able to warn the king. Or Margaret.

I will just have to find a way. Even if it meant he could be caught in the explosion, he would somehow evade Bothwell and do his duty to save Darnley from this foul plot. It was the least he could do, for one who was the God-given king of this land.

~

Bastian and Christy's wedding party was in full flow, and Margaret gazed around the room, her eyes wide at the thought that this would be happening to her too, in just two days' time. Hundreds of oil lamps and candelabra placed around the grand hall made it twinkle like some magical fairy grotto, lighting the faces of the guests as they ate and drank and laughed together.

Over in the corner, the musicians began to play a gavotte, and some intrepid party-goers formed themselves into a square, stretched out their arms and began to skip and jig in time with the lively melody. Margaret smiled to herself, remembering the time she'd danced with John at Stirling.

Then she frowned. Where *was* John?

He had been here not that long ago, although they had not been able to speak for fear of being spotted by Bothwell. Come to think on it—where was Bothwell? Circling the revellers on the outskirts of the room, Margaret scanned each face, searching for the lanky laird or the squat earl. But she found neither, and dread grew in her stomach. There was no sign of Paris, either.

"Anthony," she addressed the queen's page, who was distributing honey almonds and candied apples, "have you seen Lord Bothwell anywhere?"

"Not for a while, my lady. He were talking with that Highlander, the black-haired one. And then I think they went out." He held out the tray. "Sweetmeat?"

All the warmth left Margaret's body. She

shook her head distractedly. "How long ago?"

"Oh," he rolled his eyes heavenwards, thinking.

Margaret had to clasp her hands together to stop from shaking the boy's teeth out of his head in an attempt to get an answer out of him more quickly.

"Mayhap twenty minutes?"

Using all her acting skills to keep her expression featureless, Margaret nodded. Then she clapped a hand to her mouth as if she'd just thought of something. "Oh!"

"What is it?"

"I just realised. I left the queen's fur stole at the Old Provost's Lodging. I must go and fetch it."

"I'll get it for you, my lady," Anthony offered, "'twill be no bother."

"No, no, I will fetch it." She passed the back of her hand across her forehead. "The night air will do me good. You should enjoy the party."

"If you are sure." The page bowed, and then turned on his heel and disappeared into the throng of revellers.

Quickly, Margaret made for the door, pausing only to pick up a cloak. *I must run, or 'twill be too late.*

CHAPTER 19

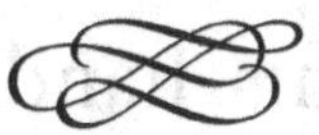

John unrolled the last of the hemp rope, his nose twitching at the musty smell of it. "There," he whispered, "that should be enough." He stood up, stretching his back.

"Enough for us to be able to get away?" Bothwell frowned at him.

"Aye. The fuse should burn for a few minutes, giving us plenty of time to escape. I can light it, if you want?"

The earl shook his head. "I'll get Paris to do it. You should go."

"Very well. Tell him to make sure the cord is burning properly before he leaves. They will sometimes fizzle out if they haven't caught properly."

Bothwell put his hands on his hips and surveyed the barrels stacked in the vaulted basement. "You are sure this is enough to do the job?"

"More than enough. It will likely take out the houses either side as well, depending on how well they are built." He hoped those houses were empty.

"As long as this one falls." Bothwell jerked his chin, then lifted his lamp higher and started towards the stone steps that led out of the wine cellar. As he passed a wooden rack filled with green glass bottles, he grabbed one with his free hand. "Shame to waste it," he said, tucking it under his arm.

When they got outside, the earl stopped abruptly, swearing under his breath.

"What?" John whispered.

"Paris. He should be on guard here." With another muttered curse, Bothwell hurried away around the corner of the building, in search of his man.

John couldn't believe his luck. Finally he was alone, and able to warn the king—before the fuse had even been set! With one last quick look behind him to make sure he was unseen, he tiptoed back into the house and hurried up the stair without waiting for his eyes to adjust to the darkness. Instead, he used the smooth wooden bannister to guide his way.

But that proved to be a fateful mistake.

At the turning of the stair, his foot caught on something—he never saw what—and he tumbled forward, a searing pain piercing his brow as his head struck the opposite rail. *The king...* But his head clouded, and that was the last thing he knew.

~

The timbered door of the Old Provost's House creaked eerily as Margaret pushed it open. She wanted to shush it to be quiet, but instead she crept in, and hurried towards the stairs. The air inside the house was still, but it had an acrid, sulphurous tang to it that she didn't remember from earlier.

She was part-way up the flight when the front door closed with a thud, a key rattled in the lock, and the bolt engaged. Her eyes widened. *I am locked in!* Then she remembered that there were windows in the king's room, and her pulse slowed a little.

With the door closed it was even gloomier inside, and Margaret cursed herself for not thinking to take a candle—but then, would a candle have been the safest thing in a house that was filled with gunpowder? Mayhap not.

At the turn of the stair, she almost tripped over something, then gasped out loud when she realised what it was. *John!* Fingers shaking, she pushed at his shoulder to roll him onto his back, and almost sang with joy when the movement caused him to puff out a breath.

Her heart began to beat once more, and she examined him quickly, using her hands, since her eyes could see little. She was reassured to feel no stickiness of blood, but he seemed to be in a stupor. "John," she whispered urgently, shaking him, "wake up!"

Groggily, he muttered at her. "Margaret. Why—"

"There's no time for that. We need to escape, and tell the king. Get up!"

Heaving at his elbow, she attempted to pull him upright, but it was like a mouse trying to move a mountain. It must have been a full minute before he was on his feet and they were headed towards the royal chamber. "What happened to you? Did someone knock you out?"

He looked sheepish. "I fell. Couldn't see where I was going."

Margaret held him tighter. It felt so good to be with him again, she had missed him so… But she could not think on that now, for they were passing through the outer chamber and about to reach the king. She stopped abruptly. "Before we wake him, I assume the gunpowder *is* here and they plan to blow it tonight?"

"Aye, in the cellar," the laird whispered back. "Could you no' smell it? They were about to light the slow fuse when I slipped away and came to warn the king." He swayed on his feet, looking like a feather would blow him over.

Grabbing John's elbow to steady him, Margaret knocked quickly on the king's door, then pushed it open, expecting to find him sleeping in the lilac four-poster.

Instead they were met by the sight of the king and his valet du chambre, William Taylor, both wearing nothing but their nightshirts. They had been standing close together at the end of the bed, but sprung apart as soon as Margaret and John entered the room. "Wh— what is the meaning of this intrusion?" the king blustered, pulling at his rumpled chemise.

"There is a plot against you, sire," Margaret explained quickly, averting her eyes from his bare legs, "they have filled the basement with gunpowder and lit the fuse. We need to escape!"

Darnley stepped towards the door. "Come, William, let us go."

"No, they have locked us in." Margaret pointed at the window. "We need to escape this way."

Quickly, she and the valet knotted bedsheets together while Darnley and the laird wrestled with the window. John was little use, still wobbly on his feet, but fortunately the king seemed to know what to do.

They tied the makeshift rope to the nearest corner post of the bed, and dropped the end out of the window. William leaned out. "'Tis long enough, it reaches the garden."

"Good." Darnley pushed him aside. "I will go first." Without further ado, he clambered onto the stone windowsill and shimmied down to the ground.

Cold night air blew in through the open window, bringing with it the smell of a midden heap from somewhere nearby, and the unearthly screech of an owl.

John looked at Margaret, in her voluminous dress, then he frowned at William. "She cannot climb, wearing that."

"Here." William grabbed the queen's purple chair. "She can sit in that and we can lower her down."

In a trice, they had fashioned a sort of cradle, fastened her into it, and somehow wrestled the contraption over the windowsill.

As she spun on the end of the rope with her eyes closed and her heart in her throat, Margaret thought that this was perhaps the most frightening thing she'd ever done—as bad as when Ember bolted and dumped her in Saint Margaret's Loch.

Half a lifetime later, she landed on the grass with a thump, sucked air into her paralysed lungs, and sent up a silent prayer of thanks.

Darnley was there—surprisingly he had not fled—to help her undo the knots, and then they tossed the chair to the side to allow John to descend.

There were a couple of moments when he lost his grip and Margaret thought that he was about to fall, but he finally made it down and almost fell into her arms.

Pushing them out of the way, the king grasped the end of the rope, gazing anxiously up at his servant. "Quickly, William."

Seeing that the king would obviously not leave until his valet was safe, Margaret led John towards the garden gate, calling back over her shoulder, "This way sire, as soon as you can."

It was not a large garden, more a patch of grass, and it backed onto a dirt track that ran down to the city walls beyond. Thankfully, it was hidden from the quadrangle the house fronted onto, so the earl and his men should not see their escape.

The latch on the gate was stiff, and, in her haste, Margaret cut her thumb opening it. But, seconds later, they were in the lane outside the garden wall, and she felt a little safer. Glancing at the laird, whose pale face and shallow breathing was concerning her, she asked, "Why has the gunpowder not gone off yet?"

"Slow fuse," he said succinctly, "hard to predict. But be careful of what you wish for. There are enough barrels to blow up half the street. We need to get away."

With a nod, she put her arm around his waist and they stumbled further up the lane, barely able to see because there was no moon in the sky. Again, Margaret cursed herself for not bringing a candle.

Behind them, she heard the gate creak, and spotted the white shirts of the king and his valet, looking like ghosts through the gloom. But, instead of following their rescuers up the track, they turned into a garden on the opposite side, perhaps thinking that was the best way to distance themselves from the coming blast.

Then the sound of pounding feet—booted feet—reached Margaret's ears over the rasp of her breath. Hastily, John pulled her into the recess of a nearby gate, putting a hand over her mouth. "Quiet," he hissed in her ear, "they may be Bothwell's men."

She nodded, and he uncovered her mouth, but still held her close. Even in this dangerous situation, she somehow felt safe in his arms, as if no harm could ever come to her when she was with him. Feeling for his hand, she gave it a quick squeeze.

At that moment, triumphant shout echoed down the lane. "In here!" A gate creaked, heavy footsteps crunched, and Margaret could almost smell the fear wafting towards them on the night air as a voice that sounded like Darnley screamed, "You cannot do—" But whatever he meant to say was silenced, and Margaret heard no more because suddenly the night sky was rent by the most tremendous explosion she had ever heard, louder even than the fireworks at Stirling.

The laird pushed her against the rough wood of the gate, leaning over her to protect her from the debris that rained down on them from the ruins of the Provost's House.

As soon as the worst of the shrapnel and flying stones had stopped, John grabbed her hand and pulled her further up the lane. "We need to get away, before they blame us," he shouted.

"Or before Bothwell's men catch us," she mouthed back.

He nodded. "That too."

Ears ringing from the aftermath of the blast, and eyes stinging from the dust that hung in the air and peppered their clothes, making them look like vagabonds, they hurried away from the scene. And then Margaret pulled at John's arm, making him stop. "What about the king?" she said anxiously, peering behind them as if she could see through the garden walls. "We should help him." She began to drag him back the way they'd come.

John's mouth set in a line, and he dug in

his heels. "I fear he is beyond help now, if that was indeed Bothwell's men. They will have smothered him, most like, to make it look like he was killed in the explosion. And I have no weapon to fight them." He gestured at his empty hip, where a sword would normally hang.

"But…" Then Margaret's eyes filled with tears, as she realised the truth of his words.

"We tried to save him, we did the best we —" Then he grabbed her hand and hissed at her, "Limp!" just as a gaggle of goodwives rounded the corner, their eyes wide and their mouths wider.

"Oh my!" said the nearest woman, pulling her apron up over her face as if to hide the scene before her. "The Provost's house—'tis gone!"

"There's nothing but rubble," said another, who had but two teeth in her whole head. "How can that have happened?"

"Sire," the third addressed the laird, her

grey hair covered by a mop cap and her face creased with concern, "are you injured?"

"Aye," said John, hobbling theatrically, "and my lady also."

Margaret took her cue, and dragged a foot as if it pained her.

"We were out—ah, taking the night air, when there was the most almighty bang. Did you hear it?" he added unnecessarily, for that was surely what had alerted the women.

"Oh yes, woke me right up it did, and I came straight out to see what happened," said the first lady, smoothing her apron back into place.

Her companion stood on tiptoe to peer over John's shoulder. "Is there anyone else hurt? Who was in the house?"

"I don't know—" John started to say, but then he was interrupted by the first woman.

"Was that not where the king was staying? Oh my!" The apron covered her face again, and she started to howl.

"We should go see, Elsie," one of her companions pulled at her arm, "mayhap he needs rescuing. Stop that noise and come wi' me."

"I must get my lady to a doctor," John spoke to their retreating backs, "but I will return to help as soon as I'm able."

"You will?" Margaret asked. "I thought we were escaping."

"They don't know that. Oh!" He spun her round to face back the way they'd come, as more footsteps echoed down the lane, and a crowd of townsfolk came up behind them, quickly overtaking them.

Margaret pulled him into the nearest garden, checked that they were not overlooked, then took out her handkerchief and began dusting the grime from her gown. "We cannot go back into town looking like this. Everyone will know where we came from."

"You are right," John said, leaning over and tousling his hair to dislodge the dirt.

"And if any of Bothwell's men see us, they will know what we did."

Two minutes later, they were almost presentable, and mingling with the crowds who'd gathered to view the site of the explosion.

As the women had said, the Old Provost's House had been razed by the blast, and only a smoking pile of stones remained to show where it had been. The sound of wailing came from the garden opposite, which seemed to confirm John's guess about the king's fate.

Margaret's eyes filled with tears again. "I must tell the queen. She will be beside herself."

John gripped her hand tighter. "You cannot tell her it was the earl. He will be sure to blame me if anyone challenges him."

"Of course. Because you provided the—"

He raised a finger to his lips. "Say it not,

lest we are overheard. We must keep this to ourselves."

Margaret jerked her chin back. "Forever?" She could not imagine keeping such a thing from her mistress.

The laird's face was grim. "Aye." A second passed, and then a smile crinkled his eyes. "But we will be married soon, and then you will be in Perthshire with me, and away from all this madness." He gestured at the gawping crowd around them. "We should be safe there."

"Forever," she said again, tasting the word on her lips.

Suddenly the terrible secret seemed less of a burden to bear. She had this wonderful man to share her life with, who would keep her free from harm, and love her always, to the ends of the earth.

It would be a new life, and it would be a better life, she was sure of it. She would be with her laird, and they would have children

—flame-haired like her, or gypsy-dark like him—and he would tend his sheep and quarry his stone while she tended house and family.

No more court intrigue. No more politics or scheming. She would be safer there, with him. She smiled to herself. Yes, everything would be fine.

Forever.

EPILOGUE

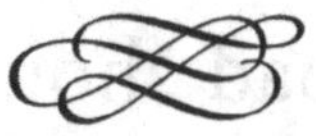

TUESDAY 11TH FEBRUARY 1567

Mary wiped a tear from her eye as John and Margaret said their vows, staring at each other like nobody else existed.

They made such an attractive couple, it was like they had been created for one another, and Mary congratulated herself for pushing them together.

The bride wore a black silk dress made in the Spanish fashion, given to her by Mary for her wedding. Against the dark gown, the autumn tones of Margaret's hair were a stunning contrast, and her milky skin glowed lustrously in the candlelight. The laird could hardly take his eyes off her.

The groom was also looking very handsome, with his broad shoulders covered in a brocade and velvet doublet and his black locks curling around his neck. He had the high cheekbones of a Highlander, and a rich voice that could be heard clearly throughout the nave.

They will make beautiful babies, Mary thought, and with that her mind turned to her own son, and the blessing that had recently been performed for them.

With growing certainty, she felt that God, in His goodness, had released her from a marriage that was not meant to be. She had trusted Him, and asked for His help, and He had given it.

She knew that she ought to be sad about her husband's death, and if she was truthful she was somewhat stunned and upset. But it was the thought that someone would hate Darnley enough to murder him that bothered her. Who would dare do such a thing to the king? It was unthinkable.

Clasping her hands, she let out a sigh. At least she could be thankful that the explosion would have killed the king—and his valet—instantly, and they wouldn't have suffered.

That was the other thing that dulled her sorrow. Despite the change of heart he'd professed to have since returning to Edinburgh, it appeared the king had not changed his profligate ways after all. Had he not been found with his valet, and both of them almost naked? Such a dalliance might explain why he didn't insist on accompanying his wife to Bastian's party.

At the altar, the priest gave his final blessing, and then the small congregation stood to watch the newlyweds process out, their first act as a married couple.

Beside her, the earl of Bothwell puffed

out his chest and lifted his chin, a slow grin spreading across his face. It seemed as if he, too, had been touched by the scene.

"I love weddings," she murmured.

He turned towards her, his eyes hooded. "Me too, my queen."

Somehow, she had the feeling there was more to his words than there appeared to be. But she found it hard to read the man, and she quickly dismissed the thought as Lady Carwood—or Lady Fincastle, as she would be now—stopped in front of the queen and dropped a curtsey. The laird, not to be out-done, gave a deep bow.

"Congratulations to you both!" Mary said. "May you be very happy together."

Margaret beamed at her. "Thank you ma'am. For all you have done. And for my lovely gown." She smoothed the skirts of the ornately embroidered dress.

"'Tis no less than you deserve for your years of faithful service. You were always my favourite lady, and I will miss you greatly. But I hope that you will have very many blessed years of marriage with your laird."

"As do we, ma'am." Margaret looked up at her husband, her eyes shining, and he lifted her fingers to his mouth and kissed her knuckles. "As do we."

THE END

A NOTE ON THE HISTORY

Of all the *Mary's Ladies* books, this story was the most difficult to write. I think that was because our hero and heroine, John and Margaret, were *real* people who did indeed marry just two days after Darnley's death (and two days after the nuptials of Bastian Pages and Christy Hogg).

The previous two books were set largely in Jedburgh, and I was desperate to move us on to Edinburgh, where Bothwell, Maitland and some other lords entered into the 'Craigmillar Bond' to kill the king.

But having John and Margaret meet at Craigmillar, at the beginning of December, and knowing they were married at the beginning of February, I had to make them fall in love and decide to get married in very short order.

In those days it was common for engagements to be short, but would a man-hating woman fall for a Highland laird that quickly, even with the queen playing matchmaker? I hope you feel I succeeded in making that part of the story believable!

TRUE HISTORY

Because of the close proximity of John and Margaret's wedding with that of Bastian and Christy, some historians have have confused the events, and have Bastian marrying Margaret. But there is written evidence that in later years he and his wife Christy were still in Mary's service.

I also found papers mentioning Margaret and John Stewart of Tulliepowries, and how they sold her half of Carwood House to her sister Janet and Janet's husband John Fleming of Persellands.

At the discovery of that text, I was rather sad, and almost had to re-write most of my first chapters. What made me sad was that John's signature was made by another hand —so he obviously couldn't write, and presumably couldn't read masque scripts either.

However, after some contemplation I decided to leave the story as it was, for John truly *was* a descendant of Robert the Bruce and Bastian *did* organise regular masques for the queen's entertainment, so it was entirely possible that it was through these masques that John and Margaret met.

SISTERS IN TROUBLE

Because they were relatively insignificant members of Scottish society at that time, there is only a limited amount known about John and Margaret, but she is recorded as one of the party of four that escaped Holyrood after Riccio's murder—read more about this by joining my mailing list and getting your copy of *A Love Departed*, which is exclusive to that group.

There is also evidence that Margaret and her sister were left as wards of Persellands after the death of their parents. He allegedly held the sisters captive for several years in their home, Carwood House, near Biggar, instead of finding husbands for them as he should have done, having received the gift of their wardship and marriage.

In 1554 when they came of age, they took the unheard-of step of taking him to court in

Edinburgh. He boldly denied the charges, but it's unknown how the case was decided.

With all of this background, I was convinced that Margaret would have been something of a man-hater, and that the man she married must have been exceptional, to change her mind—and there I had the premise for this novel!

MARY'S FAVOURITE BEDCHAMBER WOMAN

Margaret Carwood is noted in several places as the queen's favourite, and this may have been why it was *her* that accompanied Mary on the escape from Holyrood.

She joined Mary's court in 1564 (Mary only arrived in Scotland in 1561), possibly through some influence of Mary Fleming, one of the Maries and half-sister to Margaret's guardian, Laird Persellands. It is unknown what she did between 1554 and

1564, but, perhaps because of Persellands, she had not married.

It is said that the queen had some hand in arranging the marriage between John and Margaret, so I have used that in this story.

A GRIEVING WIDOWER

It appears that John may have had a child from a previous marriage (he and Margaret had four sons and a daughter). There are also records that John's family home in Perthshire, Fincastle House, was rebuilt in 1640. Nearby Bonskeid House burned down more than once, so I used this information and some artistic licence to provide his background, and his need for a wife.

Looking at ancient maps and records of the area showed that John's estate contained a lime kiln and lime quarry, so that gave me the idea of how he might have got involved in the plot to kill Darnley—the gunpowder had to come from somewhere!

Can I recommend some further reading?

FURTHER READING

For readers who are interested to know more about Mary Queen of Scots, the best books I've found are:

- *Mary Queen of Scots and the Murder of Lord Darnley* by Alison Weir
- *Mary Queen of Scots* by Antonia Fraser

GLOSSARY

Baillie: Bailiff, an officer of local government
Barmkin wall: (see Curtain Wall)
Borders (The Borders): The southern counties of Scotland, adjacent to the border with England
Bowsprit: A spar extending forward from the prow of a ship
Caliver: A light musket
Constable: The person in charge of a castle when the owner is not in residence. The caretaker

Crenel, Crenellation: Crenellations are the stepped walls of a castle, with crenels being the lower cut-outs, and merlons the higher parts

Curtain Wall: An external wall protecting the internal buildings and structures of a castle. Usually includes defensive towers

Dirk: Dagger

Ewe: A female sheep

Garron: A small, sturdy Scottish pony (see Hobbler)

Gavotte: An old French dance

Gibbet: Gallows

Glower: An angry or sullen stare

Great pox, the pox: Syphillis

Hobbler: A small, sturdy Borders pony (see Garron)

Keep: Castle or tower

Limmer: A scoundrel or rogue

Paillasse: A mattress of straw

Palfrey: A riding horse particularly suitable for a woman.

Partlet: A woman's garment covering the neck and shoulders, worn especially during the 16th century

Pavane: A dance

Pease porridge: A dish made from peasemeal, ground from yellow peas

Pend: An alleyway between houses

Piquet: A card game for two players

Port: A fortified wine. **Also**, a gate, usually within a city wall

Posset: A warm drink of wine and curdled milk

Pox: See **Great Pox**

Primero: A card game

Privy Chamber: Private room

Privy Council: A body of advisers appointed by the sovereign

Reiver: A thieving rider

Sabbath: Sunday

Thon: Scots word for *that* or *those*

Thurible: A chain censer, swung by Catholic clergy

Turnpike (gate): A barrier where a toll was charged

CHARACTERS

Names in **bold** are real historical characters.

Alexandra Cranstoun - Master of Horse to Mary Queen of Scots
Anthony Standen: Mary's page
Archibald Campbell, 5th Earl of Argyll
Bracken: Duncan's horse
Christina Hogg: Mary's servant, Sebastian Pages' fiancee
David Riccio: Mary's beloved Italian secretary, killed in March 1566

Duncan: John's manservant

Elizabeth Gordon, Countess of Huntly: Scottish noblewoman, wife of George Gordon, 4th Earl of Huntly (deceased) and mother of the 5th Earl

Ember: Margaret's horse

George Gordon, 5th Earl of Huntly

George Seton, 7th Lord Seton: half-brother of Mary Seton and Master of the Queen's household

Henry Stewart, Lord Darnley: Mary's husband and cousin

James Douglas, 4th Earl of Morton

James Hepburn, Earl of Bothwell: Member of Mary's Privy Council and Lieutenant of the Borders

James Stewart, Earl of Moray: Mary's half-brother, illegitimate son of James V, member of her Privy Council

John Fleming, 5th Lord Fleming: Brother of Mary Fleming

John Fleming of Persellands: Guardian of

Margaret and Janet Carwood; illegitimate son of Malcolm, 3rd Lord Fleming and half-brother of Mary Fleming

John Stewart of Tulliepowries, 3rd Laird Fincastle: Highland laird

Margaret Carwood: Heiress of the family of Carwood of that Ilk, and chamberwoman to Mary Queen of Scots

Mary Fleming (Flam): Lady-in-Waiting to Mary Queen of Scots

Mary Seton (Ebba): Lady-in-Waiting to Mary Queen of Scots

Mary Stuart, Queen of Scots

Nicholas Hubert, 'French Paris': Bothwell's page

Philibert Du Croc (Monsieur du Croc): The French ambassador

Robert **Nau**: French doctor. Physician to the French ambassador

Sebastian (Bastian) Pages: Valet and master of ceremonies to Mary Queen of Scots

William Maitland of Lethington: Mary's Secretary
William Taylor: Darnley's valet du chambre

ABOUT THE AUTHOR

A native Scot who lives in the hinterland between Edinburgh and the Borders, Belle loves to write about Scotland and its history.

In addition to writing historical romance, she rides dressage, teaches skiing - and pens prize-winning sci-fi, urban fantasy and contemporary romance as Roz Marshall books2read.com/rl/RozMarshall, and cozy mysteries as R.B. Marshall books2read.com/rl/RBMarshall

Find out more about Belle and her upcoming books by joining her newsletter: subscribepage.com/joinbelle

BY BELLE MCINNES, WRITING AS R.B MARSHALL:

The **Highland Horse Whisperer** series

Cozy Mystery set in Scotland (and London for the prequel):

- *The Secret Santa Mystery*
- *A Corpse at the Castle*
- *A Right Royal Revenge*
- *A Poisoning at the Pageant (due in 2021)*
- *Henchman at the Highland Games (due in 2022)*

BY BELLE MCINNES, WRITING AS ROZ MARSHALL:

The **Celtic Fey** series

Urban Fantasy / Young Adult Fantasy set in Scotland (and the faerie realm):

- *Unicorn Magic*
- *Kelpie Curse*
- *Faerie Quest*
- *The Fey Bard*
- *Wizard's Potion*
- *Merlin's Army* (releasing 30 May 2o21)

Secrets in the Snow series

Women's Fiction / Sweet Sports Romance set in a Scottish ski school:

- *Fear of Falling*
- *My Snowy Valentine*
- *The Racer Trials*
- *Snow Blind*
- *Weathering the Storm*

Half Way Home stories

Young Adult Science Fiction set in Hugh Howey's *Half Way Home* universe:

- *Nobody's Hero*
- *The Final Solution*

Scottish stories:

- *Still Waters*

BIBLIOGRAPHY

Bingham, Madeleine. *Scotland Under Mary Stuart - an Account of Everyday Life*

Campbell, Alexander, (1802). *A Journey from Edinburgh Through Parts of North Britains*

Coventry, Martin. *The Castles of Scotland*

Dunbar, John G. *Scottish Royal Palaces*

Fraser, Antonia. *Mary Queen of Scots*

Hale, John. *Mary Queen of Scots*

Harrison, John G. *The Royal Court and the Community of Stirling to 1603*

Hislop, Malcolm *How to Read Castles: A crash course in understanding fortifications*

Historic Scotland *Mary was Here: Where Mary Queen of Scots went and what she did there*

Historic Scotland *Stirling Castle: Official Souvenir Guide*

Kincaid, Alexander. *The History of Edinburgh, from the Earliest Accounts to the Present Time*

Lynch, Michael. *Queen Mary's Triumph: the Baptismal Celebrations at Stirling in December 1566*

Mahon, R.H., Major-General. *Mary Queen of Scots, a study of the Lennox Narrative*

Marshall, Rosalind K. *Queen Mary's Women*

Mikhaila, Ninya & Malcolm-Davies, Jane. *The Tudor Tailor: Reconstructing sixteenth-century dress*

Nau, Claude. *The History of Mary Stewart: From the Murder of Riccio Until Her Flight Into England*

Pearce, Michael W. *The jewels Mary Queen of Scots left behind*

Schiern, Frederik. *Life of James Hepburn, Earl of Bothwell*

Thomson, Thomas (1768-1852). *Diurnal of Occurrents - from a manuscript of the sixteenth century*

Weir, Alison. *Mary Queen of Scots and the Murder of Lord Darnley*

Yellowlees, Michael James: *Dunkeld and the Reformation*

Many web articles and wikipedia entries

ACKNOWLEDGMENTS

I am indebted to Angie, Mairi and Ben, my proofreading and beta-reading team, who added extra polish and value to my scribblings.